Left Unspoken

By Amanda Sowers

The characters and events portrayed in this book are fictitious. Any similarity to real persons, living or dead, is coincidental and not intended by the author.

Cover Designed by Q Design

For my Mom.

Who has always inspired me,
and whose story inspired this book.
I wish you were here to read it.

Friday

Hannah

I wake with a start, my clothes and hair are clinging to my body, drenched with sweat. My hands instinctively cover my mouth to muffle my cries. I can't let the sound out, to show weakness. Silent tears stream down my face as I remind myself that even though the memories are real, the dreams are most definitely not.

The night that changed my life seems like only yesterday even though eleven years had come and gone. Vivid nightmares haunted me in the years following the death of my mother but it has been a long time since I have experienced one as real as the one I just woke up from. Lately, it seems, the memories have been resurfacing with a vengeance.

I hold my breath for a moment and listen for any movement coming from the other side of my bed. My back is to him but I can hear the air leave his nose at an even pace, light snoring fills the room so I know he is sleeping peacefully. My boyfriend Matt has two responses to my nightmares, he either gets upset that I disrupt his sleep or he overlooks them completely like they don't even exist. Either way, he makes me feel like I am doing something wrong. Like these late-night terrors are my choice. Like I enjoy them.

It takes several minutes to calm myself down, even using the breathing technique that I have used hundreds of times in the past. I can't seem to get air into my lungs this time. Like the pressure will never end and I will never be able to breathe again.

When I can finally breathe normally without sobbing I

know the worst has passed, but I can't completely fight off the feeling that something bad is going to happen. The pressure doesn't completely go away, it just sits dormant, waiting.

I carefully drag myself out of bed trying not to move the bed too much, the longer he sleeps the better it will be for all of us. I ease my way off the bed, one inch at a time. Turning around to watch him, making sure my movements don't disrupt him. As I stand up something catches my eye, something is different, the closet door is ajar.

I spent most of my childhood hiding in the closet from the monsters outside, it was my safe place. As an adult, I try to avoid them at all costs. I don't want to spend my nights hiding from what I know isn't out there, I want to be free. That is why I know that I had closed the door last night. That is why I feel the need to get up and take a look inside.

There are clothes hanging from a rod that extends the length of the space, and shoes organized on the shelves to the side. The floor is mostly covered with boxes full of old memories that don't have a place anywhere in my present life. One box catches my eye, it's old and torn. Years of moving it from house to house have had its effect on it. I know it well and I know that it shouldn't be right there, in plain sight and open.

It's clear that someone has gone through it recently, was it me? I have been known to wake up in the middle of the night and do things that I don't remember. I don't know how many times I have woken up outside this exact closet, clothes torn everywhere from me apparently trying to get inside. Taking a look around I don't see anything else disturbed. Just this box.

I kneel down and finish opening the flaps of the box exposing pictures of my mother and some of the whole family from before. Hidden under the pictures are the letters I received from the police station and the prison over the years. I don't know why I even bother to keep them, something to hold onto, I guess.

Thinking about it now though, maybe having these painful reminders hidden away is actually making it worse for myself. Maybe ridding my home of the old reminders would also rid my subconscious of the painful memories that keep me awake at all hours of the night. Maybe it will help me move on once and for all.

Before I can change my mind I grab the stacks of letters out of the box, throw the pictures back and close the closet door. I quickly walk into the living room and light the gas fireplace, not waiting for regret to kick in, I toss the letters into the flames and walk away. I can smell the papers burn and can imagine all of the lies and pain that the letters hold going up the chimney with the burnt shards of paper. Chills run through me as I walk into my bedroom, somehow it feels colder now like it's missing something.

I fight off the feeling and check the time. There is still time to take a much needed long hot shower before work, but no matter how hot the water is I know that it won't wash away the feeling of disgust and hatred from my body.

My morning showers have become almost robotic. Every day it's the same, I crawl out of bed and strip my sticky damp clothes off as soon as I can. Shivering I walk into the bathroom, it's not cold in my room but fear lives in my soul these days so I can't keep the chills away. The bathroom light is motion censored, like every other light in the house, I hate walking into a dark room and not being able to see what or who is in there with me.

I avoid the mirror, I know what I will see, disheveled hair, makeup smeared all over my face, red blotchy skin from crying. There's no point in looking, it will just make me feel even worse about myself. I walk straight into the walk-in shower and waste no time turning the water on full blast, as hot as it will go. The initial impact of the burning hot water shocks my skin but after a few minutes I can no longer feel the pain, and that's how I like it.

I grab the loofah and begin scrubbing vigorously needing to wash away the sweat, shame and lack of sleep. I buy my shampoo and body wash in cheap bulk so I don't feel so guilty about using more and more as I try and scrub my skin raw. No matter how much soap I use and how hard a scrub though, I will never be clean.

As I am pulling up my pants I hear the creaking of the bed behind me, Matt is awake. My body shudders again as I quickly try and pull my shirt down to cover myself up while I wait for him to come up behind me, tensing as he does. He wraps his arms around my bare waist and snuggles his face into my neck, his facial hair scratchy against my skin. I try to continue to get dressed but I can't do much with his hands trying to get down my pants. Pushing him away, I give him a little laugh, I don't want to upset him so I play it off, hoping that he will get the hint.

Matt's a good looking man, and he knows it. His messy blonde hair, dark eyes, and perfect bone structure could make any girl swoon. He even made me swoon when we first met, something that not many guys before him were able to do. I was instantly attracted to how he dressed, the jeans he was wearing probably cost more than my entire outfit and paired with a black suit jacket he came across as very expensive. I'm not sure what he saw in me when our eyes met across the backyard at a friend's party, but he made his way over to me and just one breath of his sporty cologne had me panting like a dog.

Our relationship started out slow, most of our correspondence was done via text, it was safer that way. But against my better judgment, I started really falling for him, I think it was because for the first time in a long time I thought I had found a man that was interested in more than just what was in my pants. He seemed generally interested in every aspect of my life. We talked for hours, about everything. It was nice.

It took a few months before I let him come to the house when my daughter Quinn was home though. It's not that I didn't want him to meet her, I was just afraid that he would turn into a monster just like every other man in my life, and that was not something I was going to put my daughter through.

Once I bit the bullet and finally introduced them I was glad that I did. He seemed to fit into our lives perfectly. He was happy going to the park with us or going out for pizza with a dozen other kids, he would even just sit at home with us when we didn't feel like leaving the house. Quinn adored him and so did I. I thought maybe we had finally gotten our happily ever after. I was wrong.

We've been dating for a little over six months now and I am over his need to be the center of attention all the time. Well, when he is actually around. He seems to disappear for days at a time, which honestly is okay with me. Affection is not something I have ever experienced or even wanted before and I probably won't admit it out loud, but it all actually makes me super uncomfortable.

But it has been so long since I've had a real relationship with anyone, I don't want to give up on it without being able to say that I tried. It's not that I don't like him or he's a bad guy, I'm just not that into him, or anyone for that matter. All of my friends give me a hard time about it, telling me that I should meet a guy and have some fun while I am still young and pretty. They would never let me hear the end of it if I broke another relationship off without a good reason.

"I'm going to shower and head out. I will call you later." He pouts as he stomps away from me and into my bathroom.

His attitude about the whole intimacy thing frustrates me, but I have to remind myself that there are things he doesn't know. Things he will never know. I really should just tell him it's over but the thought is exhausting. He is going home tonight and maybe if I am lucky he won't come back for a while.

I finish getting ready, applying just enough makeup to give myself the "I didn't even try" look, and clipping some of my hair back out of my face even though I know by lunchtime it will be tossed up into a messy bun on top of my head. Walking out of my room and into the hallway I stop outside Quinn's room, listening to see if I can hear any movement coming from behind the closed door. Quinn is ten going on sixteen, and she hates mornings. As the school year goes on she seems to get used to it a little bit but it seems like every morning is a fight to leave the house.

"Quinn! We've got to get going or we will be late, again."

So far we've been late leaving the house every day this week. It literally takes four minutes to get to the elementary school from our house and for some reason, we still can't seem to get there before the bell rings. I don't want another nastygram sent home about tardies again this week. I have signed enough of those to last all year. The school district has implemented a new attendance policy and they are not afraid to let me know that we are not complying with it. I understand that attendance and being on time is something that we should be teaching our young kids but what is a few minutes? What is she missing in the two minutes she isn't there?

Quinn finally makes it out of her room and down the hall, how I don't know, she looks like she's still sleeping. Her pink shorts are wrinkled which means she probably wore them to bed last night and the shirt she has on looks as if it came off of the floor. I roll my eyes, she doesn't have time to change so it'll have to do. I hand her a cereal bar and a jacket as she walks past me right out the door. I glance at my phone, 8:19. We have six minutes until the bell rings.

Quinn's a great kid, once she wakes up, and seems to

be friends with everyone. But teenage years are approaching and the attitude that comes with it is starting to appear more and more. I am glad for the moments that her childlike innocence shows itself instead. I can't complain too much, the girl is just like me. From her moods to her looks, she's a mini-me. We share the same long black hair and pale white skin. We even have the same color of green eyes, although hers are brighter than mine are these days. We often get mistaken for as sisters, which should make me happy, but I still seem to get offended by it.

We have this strange relationship, her and I. Maybe it's because I had her so young, and we had to grow up together, but she is more like my little best friend. We are raising each other, side by side every day. I can't wait to watch how beautiful our lives become.

We sit in silence during the short ride to the school, there isn't much on the radio to listen to and Quinn's busy eating her cereal bar so there isn't much for conversation. I kind of miss when she used to talk my ear off every chance she would get. I hope that comes back, at least a little bit.

As we pull up to the school I can hear the bell ringing. It doesn't count as being late if we are here when the bell rings right? I lean over and give Quinn a kiss before she opens the door and runs after her classmates into the building. Just as she reaches the door she turns around and waves at me. We blow each other a kiss from across the playground before she continues her way inside.

As I pull away from the curb I wave to the police officer parked at the corner. The town always tries to have an officer around the schools in the morning to keep traffic under control. Some people have a hard time understanding that the speed limit is reduced around a school zone as if the crowds of children walking through the crosswalks aren't a reminder enough. The light on the corner turns yellow, knowing the police officer is right there I should probably not blow through it as I would otherwise.

As I slow the car to a stop I take a look at the police cruiser now only a few hundred feet from me, it's one of the older ones which we don't see much of around here anymore. The town is replacing them with newer models but can only afford to do one every couple of years. I didn't realize there were any of the old ones left, maybe they are using it while one of the newer ones are in the shop.

The site of the car takes me back in time. I remember that night, seeing the blue and red lights from a car very similar, as they shone through every window in my house, lighting up the room around me. The bright lights made me feel safe like they alone could save me from the nightmare my life had become.

The sudden sound of horns blaring jolted me out of my thoughts, the light in front of me is green and people have places to be. I am too embarrassed to look at the officer who probably thinks I was on my phone or taking a selfie so I just wave my hand out the window as an apology to the people behind me and ease my way through the intersection. The road I am on turns into the long highway I take to work every day, by the time I cleared the town limits my mind was wandering again.

1995

"Ready or not, here I come!" I hear my dad call out to me.

I watch from behind our big oak tree as he begins his search for me. This is my favorite hiding place, he never finds me here. I let a giggle escape from my mouth as he looks under the patio table and behind the grill. My daddy is so silly. As he picks up a small rock off of the ground and looks underneath it calling my name I can't contain my giggles anymore.

"There you are, Hannah! I thought I had lost you forever!" He says turning around.

Getting down on his hands and knees he starts crawling toward me growling like a big bad bear, which sends me into another fit of laughter and shrieks as I try to run away from him. I can't run fast enough though and he wraps me in a big bear hug and tickles me.

"Where is everyone?" My mom calls from the back door.

"Mommy's home!" I scream, running towards the house.

Mommy works weekends now leaving me home with daddy, but I don't mind. Daddy lets us eat cookies all day and always plays outside with me. Mom doesn't do these things

It's not her fault though, daddy says someone has to be an adult around here and because I am only four it can't be me. I think she's a good adult, she works all the time and that's something that adults do, right? Even when it makes me and daddy sad.

Sometimes mommy works all night long and doesn't come home until morning. That makes daddy really sad, sometimes I see him crying at night. When she comes home they fight, I guess daddy doesn't want her working so hard.

"Hannah sweetie, why don't you go wash up and change into clean clothes, we are going to go for a car ride," Mommy tells me while I give her a giant hug.

"Letty. You aren't taking her! Please don't take her."

My daddy sounds sad, but why can't I go on a car ride. Why can't he come with me? Where are we going?

"Hannah, do as you were told, I need to talk to daddy."

That means they're going to fight again. I don't want to leave him because I know he's so sad but I don't want to make mommy mad. I walk slowly down the hall to the bathroom to wash my dirty feet. Maybe that's why mommy is so mad at daddy because he didn't make me wear my shoes outside and now I am messy.

I can hear them yelling now, the walls jumble up the words so I don't know what they are saying but I know they are fighting about me. I'm not a bad kid but sometimes I do bad things.

When I get my hands and feet washed up I leave the bathroom and skip down the hallway to my room. I'm going to put on my prettiest dress, that should make mommy happy again.

Cries coming from my parent's bedroom stop me in my tracks. Why is daddy crying again? Why is mommy yelling so loud? I know the rules, I am not allowed to go in their room when the door is closed but I do anyway.

I push the door open but stop when I see that daddy has his gun out. I've seen it before when it was in the case, but I am never allowed to touch it and daddy never takes it out when I am around. Why does he have it out now?

The last thing I hear my daddy say before my mom

pushes the door closed is "I'm so sorry Hannah, I can't live in a world where I can't be your dad."

Hannah

I work as a customer representative for a local marketing firm called Hawthorne Marketing in Briar, a town located about 15 miles away from Oak Bend. The drive sucks in the winter but when it's nice out I welcome the peaceful tranquility of the open road. I put on some loud music and trust that the car will take me where I need to go while my mind is somewhere far away.

I've worked for Hawthorne Marketing for a little over five years and I couldn't ask for a better employer. The pay is great and the benefits are fantastic. There really isn't any other place around that compares to it, so I am glad that I got the job when I did. They treat all of us like family and I appreciate that as a single mother without an actual family of my own.

I moved in with my grandmother on my mom's side after my mother's death, we had always had a special bond, which is probably why she had gotten so upset when she found out that I was pregnant in high school. It took some time but we ended up coming to the agreement that we needed to raise the baby together. She was a lot of help and I could never repay her for everything that she has done for us, but we lost her to cancer a few years ago. Once she was gone I had to figure out how to do it all alone, Hawthorne made that a little easier.

Walking into the office I instantly notice the managers standing by the coffee pots, the same place they are every day when I walk in. I often wonder what they actually do here, besides drink coffee and gossip. They seem to have a lot to report on during our meetings but I don't actually see them do any work. Not enough to earn the bonuses that they do anyway.

As I walk through the maze of cubicles I wave at coworkers and mutter the occasional greeting. I don't really have friends here, considering I have worked with a majority of these people for years. We are all friendly, we say hello and goodbye, ask how their weekend went and things like that, but that's the extent of it. I don't think I have ever even seen most of these people outside of this building and definitely not on purpose. Although, I did meet the new girl Jayme in the break room yesterday and I think we made plans to have lunch today. At least I have that to look forward to.

Turning into my cubicle I can't help but notice how plain it is. I typically don't need a lot of things to get my work done but maybe I should put up some new pictures of Quinn or something. Maybe a funny quote or cat picture to help spruce it up a bit. I don't think I am a boring person but looking around I guess maybe I am. Mental note, buy things that make me look less like a loser.

The first couple hours of the day are unusually slow, leaving me plenty of time to try and find something to do. I am definitely feeling the long last couple of nights this morning, I can barely keep my eyes open as I stare at my computer screen waiting for something to happen. I have responded to all of my emails, sent a few reminders, and checked on some client issues but there wasn't much left for me to do. I'm finding it extremely hard to concentrate. I need caffeine. Checking the clock I decided that even though it's still a little early now is a good time to take a break and swing by the vending machine for a soda.

I don't have any pockets in the outfit I am wearing so hopefully I have a couple of dollar bills in my wallet. Wherever that is. I know it's somewhere in this suitcase I call a purse. As I dig through weeks of random receipts and god knows what else, I glance up and see that my manager Sara is out of her office again, has she even gone there yet this morning? Curious I try to see who she is chatting with, looks like one of the suits, someone is looking for a raise.

Feeling around in my bag again I feel something that could be a wallet, or maybe a book. It wouldn't be the first time or the last time that I found a random book in my purse. I pull it out and thank the lord that it is my wallet, caffeine here I come. As I stuff all of the loose receipts back into the bag I look up again, is that Chief Duquette that she's talking to? It sure looks like him but what is he doing out here, this isn't his jurisdiction.

I've only seen Chester Duquette a few times since he made Chief of Police a few years back. He's handsome in a grandfatherly kind of way. I notice that his full head of hair has turned grey but his eyes are just as blue as they always have been, like ice almost. I wonder how his wife is doing, she is an amazing woman, and not just for putting up with him for so many years. She runs fundraisers for the animal shelters and leads the angel tree every year too. They have two beautiful children together that are both currently out of state attending college to be something important someday. The Duquette family is perfect, I used to wish I was apart of it, I still kind of do.

I realize that I am smiling, but then I notice that they are looking back at me. I don't like the look they are giving me. Something is wrong. I can feel my hands begin to shake and my heart rate speeds up. Is it Quinn? Did something happen? I can't breathe as they make their way over to my desk.

"Hannah, please come with us. Chief Duquette needs to speak with you." Sara is trying to sound confident but I can hear the strain in her voice as she plasters a fake smile across her face.

I shove everything that I had taken out of my purse

back in it quickly, not caring how everything fits. I grabbed the bag and my jacket, not knowing if I will need it or if I will be coming back to my desk anytime soon, and follow them out of the room. Where are we going, I think to myself as we walk down the long hallway towards the meeting rooms. We stop outside one of the smaller more intimate rooms before filing inside. I notice that Officer Cleveland, the same officer from the school, is waiting for us when we walk into the room. Great, maybe this is about what happened at the stoplight, I could hope. That I could talk my way out of. That would be fine. I can't help but feel that it is something more serious than that though.

"Can I just ask what this is regarding? Is Quinn okay?" I ask the chief, my voice thick with concern.

"Hannah please sit down. Quinn's fine, but this is important." He motions to a chair beside him.

Officer Cleveland stands and pulls out a chair for me, the men wait until I am seated to sit. I am just staring at the Chief, waiting to find out what is so important. Something is clearly wrong, the chief of police doesn't just show up at someone's place of employment outside his jurisdiction for no reason. I wish he would just get on with it already. Just as Chief Duquette opens his mouth his phone rings, causing me to jump. He glances at the screen and utters a quick apology before getting up and leaving the room. Leaving me to imagine the worst in my mind. I am about to lose it when the door opens and he comes back in and takes a seat.

"The others are here, we will just give them a moment to join us," he explains as he looks at me with pity. There is a smile on his face but not in his voice, whatever he is going to tell me is not worth smiling about.

The chief has known me since the day he escorted me out of my house and into his squad car years ago. He bagged my clothes and photographed the splotches of blood that had left permanent, unseen stains all over my body. He helped with the investigation and held my hand through the months that followed. He knows more about me than almost anyone else alive, so if he came to tell me something, I know it has to be important. It has to be about that night, about our secret.

The room is silent, no one says a word while we wait for the mysterious others to join us. Who could possibly be coming in and why do we need to wait for them to get here before he tells me whatever he needs to say. Can't he see that I am going crazy over here? I look down at my shaking hands and try to will them to be still, I wipe the layer of sweat off of them on to my pants and slip them under my thighs hoping no one will be able to see the uncontrollable trembles.

The sound of shuffling feet out in the hallway makes my heart skip a beat. I know it's probably whoever the chief is waiting for and he would never put me in danger but that doesn't stop me from assuming the worst.

I'm holding my breath when the door opens, it's like everything is moving in slow motion, I can barely stand it. I let out an audible breath when three men in suits walk in. I don't know who they are or why they're here but I do know that they are not local. Oak Bend doesn't make men like that.

The one who entered the room first must be the one in charge. They all carry themselves with a confidence that screamed importance but the tall muscular man in the front gives me the impression that he has a little more say in what happens.

I stare at his perfect black suit, the way it hugs him when he moves like it was made specifically for him. I watch as he shakes hands with the chief and Officer Cleveland. I can't help but notice his perfectly white teeth when he talks and why does he have a five o'clock shadow this early in the morning? Why do I find it so attractive?

"Nice to meet you, Hannah, I am sorry that it has to be

under these circumstances. I am Agent Holder this is Agent Ridley and Agent Jackson. We are with the Federal Bureau of Investigation and we will be assisting with this case." The hot one says as he shakes my hand.

I am startled by the electricity that flows through us when our hands touch. Wait, what did he say? Agent Holder with the FBI? What is the FBI doing here and what case is he talking about? The look on my face must give away my confusion because the agent turns and looks at the chief questioningly like I should know what's going on and why they are standing in front of me right now.

I turn to the chief too, he was supposed to have told me something already. What is he not saying?

"What's going on Chester?" I demand.

"Hannah," Agent Holder speaks first kneeling down beside me. "I am sorry to have to be the one to tell you this but the man who murdered your mother escaped from prison this morning."

Mark Patterson

Escaping from prison is not something that I expected to be planning to do, I didn't spend my free time trying to figure out how to break out of cell 13 in block C. Not that the thought didn't cross my mind in the last eleven years since they threw me in here and tossed away the key. I definitely had more than a couple of late-night thoughts about what it would be like to walk out of this hellhole. I just never had a real plan until now.

They told me from the start that I had the right to appeal my sentence, which I had done, with no success. I quickly learned what they don't teach you in school, the justice system is not very just. They told me that I was lucky that I didn't receive the death penalty, an eye for an eye they said. I often wonder if death would have been the better option, but they are wrong, it's not what I deserve. They don't understand that I did what I had to do, I didn't have a choice. Because they don't understand my actions they assume that what I did was wrong. I wasn't wrong. They were. They never even found the gun, they had no case against me.

I don't think my attorney is very good at his job, and for what I am paying him he should be very good. We had met several times to prepare for the appeals but when the last one came back affirmed the meetings almost stopped altogether. We were running out of options and we both knew it. We didn't have much else to talk about. When he was here last I think we both knew it was going to be the last time.

He seemed distant, the positive glow that he had early

on in the process was no longer there and he talked like we had already lost. He was sorry. Not as sorry as I was for wasting my time and money on such a pathetic loser. I may have lost my temper for a moment but he was saved by a call that he had to take. Cell phones are annoying, how they let them pass through security I will never know.

He took the phone with him and left the interview room to take the call somewhere a little more private. Once he was gone I decided to get my monies worth anyway and look through the files he had brought with him. After all, they had my name on them, I think I had the right to look at them.

The first few pages were just shitty notes from the appeal, which kind of pissed me off again, but then things got interesting. The photos. The first few I had seen before, crime scene photos that showed the bloody aftermath of the shooting. The living room where my wife was shot, the hallway walls smeared with blood from Hannah, and the kitchen floor littered with broken glass.

Thinking about that night makes me upset. I can remember it so vividly; the last time I had ever touched the love of my life. Begging the police officers to let me see her, but the bastards just ignored me. They treated me like a monster, but I am not the monster, love just makes you do crazy things.

Sitting there looking at those pictures brought up a lot of emotions and that's when I realized that I couldn't wait for the appeal to be denied again, I had to do something to make sure Hannah was okay. I have been gone for too long, it was time to plan our reunion.

I didn't even wait for my useless attorney to return, I had the guards take me back to cell block C where the planning could really begin. I knew which guards I could get to mail out letters without checking them first, I would need to get some out to a source I had on the outside. He would track Hannah's movements so she could be easily found when the time came. I would need a car and a place to stay, all of which would come at a price, a high price.

Fortunately, my piece of shit dad left me a good amount of money when he kicked the bucket a few years back and my little brother Ray would do just about anything that I told him to. He would be glad to help his big brother break out of prison. Even if he wasn't happy about it he still would, or he knew what could happen. Ray wasn't very smart but he definitely wasn't stupid.

I'm older than Ray by about thirteen years. We were never really close as kids. I was an only child, the center of my mother's world and then she got pregnant again. I was heartbroken, she didn't need another kid, she had me. My heartbreak went unnoticed as her stomach began to swell and everything revolved around her and her miracle baby. It wasn't my fault that she chose the baby over me.

She was three weeks shy of her due date when I got so mad at her I accidentally pushed her a little too hard, too close to the steps. She didn't fall all the way down, but when she got up there was a bright red puddle on the floor. Blood was seeping down her legs as she begged me to call 911. I did, but it was too late. They were able to deliver Ray safely, but our mother lost too much blood. Ray took my mother away from me. I had been robbed of the first woman I ever loved, and I vowed that I would never allow another piece of my heart to be ripped out like that again.

Hannah

"Escaped! What do you mean escaped? He is in a maximum-security prison!" I am panicked. Filled with shock and confusion.

Mark Patterson had confessed to murdering my mother in cold blood over a decade ago and had been rotting in the South Dakota State prison ever since. The last thing I ever expected to hear was that he had escaped.

"He was accounted for at breakfast but when he didn't show up for his shift in the library it raised alarm. A complete lockdown was initiated and the grounds were searched but he wasn't located." Agent Ridley explains.

"How did this happen? Is he coming here? Does he know where I am?" I can't even think straight with so many questions coming to mind.

"We have reason to believe that he may come looking for you. We don't have all of the details but the Department of Corrections is investigating, trying to gather more information." Agent Holder finally replies.

Chief Duquette takes my other hand and looks long and hard at me, squeezing my hand gently. He had become almost like a father to me during the rough few months following the murder, he had gone above and beyond during the investigation. This has to be hard on him as well.

"We are going to take you and Quinn into protective custody until he is back where he belongs. He will not hurt you again. I promise." he sounds confident.

I can't even form words through my shock. How could

this be happening? The man destroyed my childhood, my whole life, and now he's back. This time I have Quinn to worry about. The thought of Quinn sent chills up my spine.

"Does he know about Quinn?" I barely whisper the question.

"We have no reason to believe that he would know that you have a child." I think he is going to say more but he doesn't.

"I know this is a lot to take in but we should get going. We called the school and they have Quinn ready to go, we will pick her up on our way to the station. We also called Matt, he will meet us at the station." He stands before he is finished talking.

"You called Matt? How did you even know about him?" I'm confused.

"It's my job to know about things like that Hannah. He wasn't happy about the call though, so I can't promise he will stay." He doesn't seem concerned by this.

It's not actually surprising to me, Matt doesn't really care about anything, except maybe what's in his pants and getting into mine. Actually, I'm not sure it's my pants he cares about getting into, as long as he can get into someones. I can't believe I didn't even think about him this whole time, is he in danger too?

I feel something wet hit my hand, a tear, I am crying. I never cry this is too much. I can't breathe in this small room with everyone staring at me, but what's outside that door? Mark's out there. He could be right outside waiting for me. Has he had enough time to get this far yet? I don't know, but I do know besides the people in this room there was no security in this building and I need to make sure Quinn is safe. Suddenly I am in a hurry to get out of this room, but I stand too fast and start to stumble. Great now I am going to fall on my face, maybe they'll just leave me there.

Luckily for me, the agents all stood at the same time I

did and Agent Holder caught me right before I embarrassed myself any further. Not letting go of my arm he grabbed my bag and led me out of the room as we followed the chief down the hallway. I can't breathe and at this point, I am not sure if it's from the news that I had just heard or because of the man that was very close to me. Either way, I needed outside, now.

A rush of fresh air hits me as we walk out the door, it feels nice on my tear-streaked face. I can finally breathe again, I stop to try and take all the air in but after a few moments I remember who could be out here with me. The agent must have noticed my shutter and the look of panic hit my face again because he has started to lead me to a black Escalade parked near the door. Opening the door for me he continues to hold on to my arm as I climb into the backseat if it was any other time I would probably be flattered by his actions but I just want to leave, I want to see Quinn.

The drive back to Oakbend takes about ten minutes, but it feels like an eternity as horrible memories start to invade my mind. Suddenly I am that scared little girl again, hiding from my own personal monster in the back of a closet. Shaking my head I try to clear the memories away, bright blue eyes in the rearview mirror caught my attention. Agent Holder is watching me, smiling reassuringly.

As we pull up in front of the elementary building I can't stop the chills from climbing up my spine, there are children inside that have no idea what kind of monsters exist in this world, but what's worse is that there are some that do. I am shaking as the chief opens my door and helps me out of the vehicle and leads me up the path to the school.

Quinn jumped up to hug me when we walked in, I need to reassure her that everything is okay. How can I do that when I know that that is a lie? I force my best fake smile and hug her back. I never want to let go of this little girl. The chief must have briefed the school well because they don't ask any questions, I watch the principal wave at Quinn as we walk out the door. I can't bring myself to wave back or return his smile. He has a better poker face than I do.

The agents are all standing outside the Escalade when we return to the vehicle, they appear to be looking over their shoulders and keeping an eye on everything. That doesn't ease my concern any. I usher Quinn into the backseat with me, I don't want her outside any longer than she has to be. As soon as we are all back in the vehicle Quinn starts telling me about her morning, I can't seem to concentrate on what she's saying but I am relieved when I notice that the agents seem to be engaged in her story. Someone needs to be, I can't even think straight. Am I supposed to be sad, upset, scared? I'm just numb.

Finally, I see the police station come into view, we are almost there. Looking out the window, I notice that there are news vans in the parking lot, the agents must have noticed too. I hear one of the agents swear under his breath which causes Quinn to giggle. We follow the chief past the parking lot and through a back entrance which leads to an open garage door. Once we drive inside, the door closes leaving us inside a large parking garage. We are finally safe. I hope.

1995

My daddy doesn't live with us anymore. Mommy said he went to live with Jesus, but I don't understand why he would do that, it must have made him really sad to leave us. I know it made me really sad.

Mommy doesn't work as much anymore. I like having her home but she isn't as much fun as daddy was. Daddy's friend Mark has been here a lot. Helping out around the house and making sure mommy doesn't get lonely. She said Mark is going to be my new daddy, but I don't want a new daddy I want my old dad back. Mark's nice and will make a great daddy to someone someday but not me.

Mark is bigger than my daddy. Taller and more muscles. I think he's kind of scary but mommy says there is nothing to be afraid of and I need to be a big girl now. She said now that I'm almost five I can't cry so much. I know it makes her upset when I cry so I'm going to try not to do it so much anymore.

Mommy is pacing around the living room in front of the window waiting for Mark, it's what she is calling "Move-in day." She's really excited I can tell. I just wish it could be just me and her.

"Hey, there's my girls!" He calls walking into the house wrapping my mom into a hug.

I look away when they kiss, old daddy didn't get kisses from mommy, why does new daddy get them?

"Hannah. Say hello to Mark." Mommy scolds me.

"Hi, Mark," I whisper.

"Hey, Hannah girl. I know this is new and going to take

some getting used to but I promise this is going to be a good thing." Mark tells me.

I smile, I don't believe him but I hope he's right. I'm tired of being sad and maybe having Mark here will make mommy happier too.

"Hey, pretty girl I have a surprise for you. Want to see it?" He asks.

A surprise? I love surprises. I wonder what it is. I jump up off of the floor where I was playing nodding my head excitedly.

"Well c'mon then." He calls heading through the kitchen to the back door.

I run after him, not able to contain my excitement. When he opens the patio door I stop. I can't believe what I am seeing. On the deck in front of me is the prettiest pink bicycle I have ever seen.

I can't even speak right away. Is it for me? I've never had my own new bike before. My old bike used to belong to the neighbor boy and it wasn't pretty at all. I used it to learn how to ride without training wheels but I always wanted my very own bike.

"Hannah. Don't be rude. Thank Mark for his gift." My mom scolded me again.

"Sorry. Thank you!" I told him through a big smile.

"Let's take it down to the sidewalk so you can ride it," Mark says taking my little hand into his.

Maybe having a new daddy won't be so bad after all.

Hannah

The police station is buzzing with activity when we walk in. I don't think this small town has ever seen this much excitement, at least not in the last eleven years. Everywhere I look I see people. Some of them wearing uniforms some in suits, but they all look important and busy. It's warm in here and my head is spinning, everyone is running around and it's making me dizzy. I hold on to Quinn's hand a little tighter to make sure she stays next to me and doesn't get lost in the mess. Finding a couple of empty chairs I lead her over to them and we take a seat and wait.

From where we are sitting I am able to see Agent Holder and the other agents deep in conversation across the room. I can't make out what they are saying but it looks like it's getting intense. It's hard to concentrate on them with the noise level of the room. It's like there's a constant buzz ringing in my ears.

"Hey, here's something to drink and some snacks if you're hungry." The words startle me, I didn't realize the chief had come up beside us.

"Thanks. What do we do now? What if they don't find him? Chester, I'm scared." I try to keep my voice down, I don't want Quinn to hear me.

"We are preparing a secret safe house for you to be moved to where you will be more comfortable while we wait it out. Only a handful of people will know where you will be, so we know that you are safe. I want you to know though that there are a lot of people working on this. You are safe here and we will find him." he replies, scanning the room with his eyes.

The agents join us at the table with some paper and crayons, Agent Jackson asks if Quinn would like to join him on the other side of the table to color. I appreciate that he is trying to keep her busy and away from all of this. As they move to the other side of the table agent Holder takes a seat next to me where she was sitting. He doesn't say anything he just sits quietly next to me. I'm thankful for that, I am not sure I could hold a conversation right now.

Suddenly I can feel him tense beside me, there is a change in the room, it's like the air got a little thicker making it harder to breathe. I look up to see what was going on and notice that Matt is talking to the chief just outside the door. I don't want him here, as he walks up to me I am not even trying to hide the disappointment on my face. He doesn't seem to notice, or he just doesn't care. He wraps his arms around me and kisses me a little too long. I all but push him away from me with frustration. He doesn't seem to notice that either. He is too busy making sure the agents and everyone else in the room know that I am his.

"When they told me you were here, I came right away. Is everything okay?" He fakes concern well.

"Hannah and Quinn could be in danger, so as a precaution, we are keeping them in protective custody until further notice. We would like if you remained in custody as well, for your protection." Chief Duquette says, with a little less concern, he is clearly annoyed.

I wait to see what Matt will say and after a few seconds, I am shocked by his reaction. He is laughing out loud and it's kind of creepy. Does he think this is a joke? The way he is looking around makes me wonder if he really does think it is. Everyone in the room is now staring at us, well at him but I am sure they are looking at me too, after all, he is here with me.

"I heard about the escape on the radio, you can't

honestly believe that he would come here looking for her, can you? If it were me I would be halfway to Hawaii by now. There is no way he is coming back here to this shithole, Hannah isn't worth getting caught again. Babe, get up, we are going home."

Everyone is watching us like we are some sort of circus act or something. No one makes a sound as they wait to see what I will do next. I kind of wish someone would step in and tell him no, or make him leave. No one does, so I guess I have to.

"No Matt, they brought you here for your protection! You don't have to stay, in fact, I prefer it if you don't. I am going to do what I need to do to make sure Quinn is safe. He may not come back here and I really fucking hope that I am not worth it, but he is an animal and who knows what he is thinking right now. So I am staying, and you are going home. Not to my house, but to your own." I am really trying to remain calm, but who the hell does he think he is?

"No, you don't get to tell me what to do. Damn right I am leaving but if I walk out that door without you then it is over, we are done." He's still yelling, getting closer and closer to me with each word.

"Okay, that's quite enough. You're free to go now. If you need help finding the door I will be happy to walk with you." Agent Holder growls at him. That was definitely a threat.

There is no way Matt is going to let the agent get away with talking to him like that but I don't get to hear what else is said as all three of the agents are following him out the door.

"It'll be a little bit yet until we can get you guys into the safe house, we are double-checking the security and making sure everything is ready for you." Chief Duquette says, trying to change the subject.

I give him a nod, not sure what else to do or say. While we wait, I watch the people in the room. There are still so many of them. I can hear the phones ringing and people talking loudly but I can't understand what any of them are saying. I have to just believe that they are doing everything that they can to protect us. I just wish that they would update me or tell me something. I am losing my mind sitting here, I need a break.

"Hannah?" Agent Holder is suddenly sitting next to me. "I know this is all probably overwhelming, there are a lot of people in here, but I want you to know they are the best possible people to get this done."

"You already know Ridley, Jackson and of course the chief here." He continued. "Those two gentlemen on the left with the laptop are US Marshals working with the PD on roadblocks, and searching vehicles coming into town. Assisting them with that are those agents over there," he explains as he points out another group of people in the room. "Those three men over there are talking directly with agents that are working with the Department of Corrections to figure out how this happened. And the two men that just left the room complete your protection team. We are specifically here to make sure you're still alive when Mark gets thrown back into his hole. So don't die." He says with a straight face, but then turns and gives me a wink.

"I will do my best." I can't help but laugh at his attempt at a joke.

"Good. You know what I think, while we wait for all of these people to do their thing, we just eat junk food and watch movies. Because under the protection of the Federal Bureau of Investigation you two will be safe. There is nothing for you to worry about, let them do the worrying." He says, scanning the room around them.

Even with his impressive speech the thought of the safe house really makes me nervous, won't the police station be safer? I glance over at Quinn who's still sitting across the table, she's coloring a picture of a dog, seemingly oblivious to everything around her. Maybe it would be best to get her out of here. She doesn't need to be in the middle of all of this, she needs somewhere to play and needs real food.

While we wait for our next instructions, I decide to pull up a movie for Quinn on my phone and we sit down together to watch it. Well, Quinn watches the movie while I try to gather my thoughts. I can't believe Matt acted like that, but to be honest, if they had asked me, I would have told them not to call him at all. Even with all of this going on around me I am embarrassed that he behaved like that in front of the agents.

He has always been that way though, he always makes me feel like I am being overdramatic any time something from my past comes up. Like I should be over it by now and forgive Mark for destroying me. He seems almost annoyed that it bothers me so much. He wasn't like that at first, in fact, when we first met he seemed almost obsessed with the details. Then time went on he cared less and less until I couldn't even mention it in front of him without him getting upset.

He wasn't always bad, I recall the night we met and how he made me feel. It was like yesterday, thinking about it now I can almost feel the chill of the night air against my bare skin. The memory of better days pulls me in as the buzz of the room lulls me into a daze.

"Hannah! C'mon, it's my last birthday party in Oak Bend. You promised you would have fun." My best friend whines.

"I am having fun, I just need some fresh air. Go back inside and have fun with your other guests. I'll be right in." I reassure her.

I watch as she pretends to pout before she turns around and dances her way back to the house. I'm going to miss her when she's gone. We've been friends for a few years now but she got an amazing job offer in another state and will be moving in a couple of weeks. I'm so happy for her but I wish she wasn't leaving.

When she reaches the sliding glass door she turns around and blows me a kiss. "Hurry up loser!" She calls as she walks through the door into the house.

I should go inside and enjoy the party. It took a lot of work to get me here tonight. I had to find a babysitter, buy a new dress, and I spent so much time on my hair and makeup. I have to admit though, I do feel great. Beautiful even, for the first time in a long time. But I do miss Quinn, and my comfy bed, and Netflix.

I almost have myself talked into going and telling the birthday girl a little white lie and a sweet goodbye when I am sidetracked by a stranger walking out of the patio doors. He's on his cell phone and doesn't seem to notice my obvious gawking. I hope he doesn't anyway.

As he paces back and forth across the patio it's hard not to stare at the way his jeans hang on his hips. How he looks in his black button-up shirt with the suit jacket over it, but what I notice above all of that is his confidence. He carries himself like he knows he is hot as fuck, and I can't get enough of that.

When he hangs up the phone he notices me for the first time and stops in his tracks. He just stands there and stares at me for a moment, a cocky grin on his face.

"Why is the prettiest girl at the party outside all by herself?" He asks.

"Whatever." I giggle like a little girl. "There are plenty of better-looking girls inside." I can't help but be flattered.

I watch in awe as he struts towards the patio chair that I am sitting in. As he gets closer a light breeze picks up the scent of his cologne and I feel my body reacts to the woodsy smell even before he takes a seat in the chair next to me. I try not to let him see how his presence is affecting me but it's hard to do that when he's practically touching me.

"So why are you sitting out here instead of enjoying the party?" He asks curiously.

I take a deep breath and turn my attention to the

stranger now sitting beside me. Now that he is closer, much closer, I notice the color of his eyes. They are intense, like a cloudy night sky. The dark blue and grey dance together in the most intoxicating way, I find myself lost in them.

"Do I have something on my face?" He asks laughing while rubbing the stubble on his face.

"Uh... What? No, sorry. I guess I'm feeling the effects of the wine." I stumble through the words while playing with my half-full glass of wine.

"That's okay. You don't do this very often do you?" He asks. "Forgive me if I'm way off here but you seem more like the kind of girl who prefers to stay home on the weekends." He adds quickly.

"You're not wrong. I can't even remember the last time I went out. The only reason I am here tonight is that Tosh is my best friend and she guilt-tripped me into coming." I admit. "I was actually just thinking about faking a babysitter emergency so I could go home."

"Babysitter emergency?" He looks confused as he continues. "You have kids?"

There it is, I shouldn't have said that. I should have let his moment last a little bit longer. I haven't had a man call me pretty in so long, I wish I could let this go on all night and just see where it leads us.

"Just one, a girl. She's ten. Sorry for wasting your time." I say standing up.

"What do you mean? You're not wasting my time. Just let me know if there's a husband or a boyfriend though so I can turn down the charm. I don't want to get my ass kicked tonight." He smiles.

"No, it's just the two of us, but she can get a little feisty." I joke.

"Matt!" Tosha yells coming towards us. "You're the reason my best friend in the whole world isn't inside at my birthday party?"

"Happy Birthday girl!" He stands to wrap her in a giant

hug.

I spark of jealousy hits me for just a moment before I remember that Tosha is engaged to be married to an amazing man. There is nothing to be jealous of. They must be friends.

"Hannah, how do you know Matt?" She asks me excitedly.

"I don't," I admit. "We just met."

"Oh my gosh, you will love him! He is so fun! Matt is Josh's friend from high school he lives out of town and I didn't know he was even going to be here today. You idiot, why didn't you tell me?" She shrieks.

"It was really a last-minute decision. Once I knew for sure I could make it I wanted to surprise you! I hope you're surprised, Tosh." He leans in and kisses her softly on the cheek.

"I am! Thank you so much for coming! Josh is inside you should go find him. I need to go dance with my Hannah Banana!" She grabs my hand and drags me towards the door.

I am suddenly startled out of the memory when I feel a light tap on my arm. The agents have returned and I probably look stupid with drool running down my face.

"Hannah, It's time to go." I hear, but I am not sure who actually said it.

I quickly gathered our things and we make our way back out of the station and into the parking garage. I see the black government-issued SUV that we came in and assume that we will be taking that again, but as I follow the agents I realize that we are walking right by it and towards a white van instead. On the side of the van is the name of a local electric company, I've seen these vans all over town.

The agent opens the back door and indicates that we should climb inside, I am pretty sure I have been told several times not to get in the back of a white van, for any reason. I can't help but giggle a little bit at the situation. I am getting into a creepy white van to keep myself safe, I am not sure that has ever been done before. I feel like I should be looking for free candy.

Once inside I help Quinn buckle her seatbelt and then take my seat to buckle my own. I don't see any candy but I do see a pretty complex looking computer system that takes up an entire sidewall of the van. They must use this for undercover, I have to admit it's actually kind of neat. If I was sitting here for any other reason I might actually find it fascinating.

"This is Jim, he is going to be taking us to a really cool house where we can eat pizza and watch Netflix!" pointing towards the man in the driver's seat of the van Agent Holder makes introductions.

That was enough to win Quinn over. She smiles at me and whispers how excited she is to be hanging out with the FBI. I thank the lord that she doesn't understand what is actually going on. I have a feeling she is going to find out soon enough, but until then I want to hang on to whatever innocence she has left. I don't want her to turn out like me.

I look ahead and notice that Agent Holder is looking at me, he gives me a smile and a nod before turning around to face the front of the van. His blue eyes and a friendly smile have a way of calming me. I mean, that's his job right? He's here to protect us, and once Mark is back behind bars, he will leave. I shouldn't get too attached to the warm feeling I get when he flashes his incredible smile at me.

Mark

The escape went off without a hitch, just like I had planned. I made sure that everyone got a good look at me in the morning, all the guards knew exactly where I was at all times. Then on my way to my shift working in the library, I just disappeared without a trace, or at least that's what they will all believe. Except for the guard that got a hell of a paycheck to move the camera in the back hallway, and mistakenly leave the back door propped open. It should have been harder than that, but it wasn't. I walked right out the back door and into the trunk of a waiting car.

Except for the guard that I had chosen was supposed to be too stupid to figure out that he was just a pawn in all of this. I didn't think that he would realize that I had power over him, I definitely wasn't expecting to be blackmailed by the idiot. When the man confronted me demanding more money for his silence I had to suppress a laugh, right before breaking his neck. I didn't want to have to kill him, he was a nice guy, but he was in the way. No one was going to stand in my way, not today.

So now here I am with no plan, no car and nowhere to go. How did I not think this would happen? I guess prison has really messed with my mind, I thought I had the upper hand. Pacing around the apartment of a now-dead man, I think of a new plan. I will have to take his car, just to get out of town then dump it when another one becomes available. I have to get to Oak Bend where Hannah is, I can find somewhere to stay there. Changing out of my prison jumpsuit I grab my burner phone and the keys to the car and head out the door.

I decide to get on a dirt road to avoid any roadblocks or being spotted by people that were on the lookout for me. Just as I clear city limits and begin breathing easy again I spot a police cruiser sitting on the side of the road ahead. Shit. I check the speedometer but I don't know what the speed limit actually is out there. I am sure things have changed in the last eleven years. I slow down to 55, which seems like normal speed. As I drive past the cruiser the cop flips his lights on and pulls out behind me.

I pull the vehicle over to the side of the deserted dirt road muttering a curse word my breath. I don't have time to panic I need to do what needs to be done. I roll down the driver's side window when the officer climbs out of the cruiser. The officer doesn't seem suspicious as he casually approaches the vehicle, so he must not be looking for me. That makes me relax a little. It's just a routine traffic stop, unfortunately for the cop it's going to be the last one he will ever make.

The officer smiles as he approaches my window, clearly not suspecting to be face to face with a convicted murderer. I watch as he bends down to talk to me, not yet realizing that he has made a terrible mistake by choosing to pull me over today. Smiling at him I try to play it cool.

"Is there a problem here officer?"

With a professional smile on his face, he looks in the car through the window and checks the backseat.

"You were going a little fast back there, these back roads have a lot of loose gravel and some wicked curves. I just want to make sure everyone stays safe."

"Sorry sir, I am from out of town, I wasn't sure what the limit was. I will be more careful."

"I understand, no harm is done. How about I just check your license and registration and then we can both be on our way. How does that sound Mister? What's the name again?"

I could lie to him and make up a name, give him some bullshit story about how I left my wallet at the hotel and hope that he moves on, but I know that that is unlikely. He won't let me just drive away without showing him some sort of identification or at least running the name that I gave him. So I do the sensible thing, I tell him the truth.

"Mark Patterson."

The look of recognition on his face is undeniable, in a split second he makes a crucial mistake, he freezes before reacting, which gives me plenty of time to swing the door open and knock him off his feet.

Before he even hits the ground I am out of the car and on top of him swinging, my fist connects with the bridge of his nose right away, I can feel the undeniable crunch as the bone gives away, spraying blood across the pavement. The hit stuns him long enough for me to make my next move. Reaching for his service weapon in his holster at his hip before he even realizes what I am doing. I grab the gun and point it right at his big dumb bloody head breathing heavily, I stumble into a standing position in front of him.

Even the prison weight room has not prepared me for this type of adrenaline, I can barely catch my breath as I wonder what I am about to do next. I can shoot him in the leg, he'll probably live but I will have time to get away. I don't want to kill the man, his only mistake was getting in my way. But if I kill him he won't be able to tell anyone what happened, they wouldn't suspect me right away, would they?

"Please! I just got married! My wife, she's my whole world. We just bought a house, we are trying to have kids. We want a lot of kids. She's going to be such a good mom. I need to go home to her tonight. Please let me go home to her."

I look down at the man again, it's almost pathetic the way he is begging for his life, maybe I can let him live and go back home to his pretty little wife, or maybe she can find another man who isn't such a baby. A laugh escapes my lips at the same time the bullet leaves the gun. It's quick but the swift movement leaves blood and brain matter splattered against the road covering it in a deep crimson color that runs under the car and into the ditch.

Looking down I swear again, out loud this time, no one is around to hear me anyway. My new jeans are covered in blood. After 12 years of wearing various oversized jumpsuits, I can't even wear casual clothes for more than an hour without destroying them. It's okay Hannah will wash them for me, she will take care of me just like I have always taken care of her.

I take another look at the man in front of me, a coward, I spit at him before walking away. I open the door to the car and dig around in the backseat to see if there is anything I can use to wipe the disgusting shit off of my clothes. Why is there so much shit back here? Did this man ever clean? There are wrappers and empty bottles littered all over the floor. Just as I am about to say fuck it I find a dirty towel stained with something brown and disgusting, I don't even want to know what he used this for, but it will have to work.

I toss my new gun onto the passenger seat next to the burner phone and climb back into the car. The gun may come in handy later. Not that I want to have to use it but I am starting to think that there are going to be a lot of people that step in my way.

Leaving the dead body in the middle of the road I drive away, glancing in the rearview mirror and watching as the lights from the cop car fade away into the distance. I'm going to need to ditch this car more sooner than later. It won't take long for them to come to check on why the cop is not responding to his radio and what they will see are this car and my ugly face. They are probably trying to reach him already, he isn't going to be responding. All it will take is for them to pull his dashcam to see my ugly ass shoot him in the head.

It isn't long before I catch sight of a yellow house coming up along the side of the road. It isn't a huge house but it appears to be well taken care of I would have to bet there is someone living there. Hopefully someone stupid enough to leave their keys in their vehicle.

I check the rearview mirror to make sure there is no one else on the road before pulling my car gently into the ditch and up through a break in the trees, concealing it from anyone who may pass by. Getting out of the car I back away from it slightly to make sure that I am satisfied with the hiding spot.

Leaning back into the open door of the car I grab the phone and the gun, tucking it into the waistband of my jeans before walking away. I can see the house from here through the trees, but I don't think that they will be able to notice the car if they are not looking for it. The trek towards the house is muddy and the overgrown weeds scratch my arms as I walk through them, but there isn't a long way to go.

As I make my way to the clearing, I see a young boy and a dirty white dog running back and forth through the tall grass in the yard. An older man, I assume is the boy's father, is on the broken up cement driveway toying with a lawnmower. It appears that he is having a hard time getting it started. The idiot can't even use a lawnmower, I just hope that the truck behind him runs.

I don't want to have to kill the man in front of his son, and I definitely don't want to kill the boy but there's a good chance that I won't get away with the truck if I don't. I almost regret having the thoughts, maybe there is another way. I ponder for just a moment, but I know that there aren't many other options, so before I change my mind I pull the gun out and make way into the yard towards the man. I get almost all the way into the yard before I am spotted by the dog, his barking gives away my position.

As the man looks up, I don't hesitate to take the shot, hitting him in the chest. He falls backward, almost in slow motion as blood pools around him. He is still moving but I don't immediately take another shot. The young boy starts screaming and the dog is going crazy. His loud shriek of bark and the kid screaming is all I can hear the sound fills my head. I can't stand the sounds any longer, I don't even realize what I am doing until I pull the trigger and the dog falls to the ground with a loud yelp. I point the gun at the kid who is screaming even louder now, he seems more upset about the dog than his own dad. I lower the gun for a moment, then turn and pull the trigger one last time, putting a bullet between the eyes of the man on the ground. He's dead now. He didn't have to be, he could have just let me take the truck, he could have stayed out of my way.

The kid will probably thank me someday when he realizes what his life can be without his worthless father. Looking at the boy one last time, I walk over to the truck and climb inside. Reaching over to start it a jolt of panic hits me when I realize the keys are not in the ignition. I quickly scan the front seat of the vehicle and spot them laying on the passenger seat. I mutter thanks before shoving the keys into the starter and turn it over listening to the purr of the engine. Fuck, I am glad that started. I waste no time tearing out of the driveway sending rocks flying across the yard. I don't look back, I already know what I would see, a sad boy and his pathetic dead father.

I know that I can't stay on this road it will be loaded with cops in no time. The fact that I haven't seen one or heard any sirens surprises me, maybe they haven't checked in on the young officer yet. I see a minimum maintenance dirt road ahead, it looks like a muddy mess but I kick the truck into four-wheel drive and swing onto the road. The tires sliding all over and the engine revving as it fights its way through. I don't think anyone will try following me down this road. I take another couple of turns for safe measure, hopefully, no one will find me out here.

I drive for several miles before I see a small dilapidated house with a short driveway overgrown with weeds. The white paint was peeling and the roof looked like it was beginning to cave in. I bet it's empty, no one in their right mind would live in this house. I can hide out here until I get the call about my girl.

Opening the front door to the house was harder than it should have been, I had to kick it open. When I got into the room I am surprised by a little old lady staring at me from the kitchen. Shit. I have to kill someone's grandma. She isn't hard to subdue though, being old and fragile made it easy for me to break her neck. I feel bad immediately, she didn't deserve to die. I find a bedroom and carry her inside, tucking her nicely into the bed before walking out shutting the door behind me.

So now I wait here in this empty house waiting for a phone call that will bring my girl back into my life. I know there are a lot of people looking for me out there, but no one knows where I am. Hopefully, they give up the searches soon then we can be free.

Chief Duquette

Watching as the van pulls out of the garage taking Agent Holder and the girls to the safe house makes me breathe easier. Soon they will be tucked away into a house in the middle of nowhere, where no one could find Hannah and more importantly no one could question her. The safe house has never been used for a case like this, in fact, it has never been used for a case at all. The county had acquired the house after the previous owners failed to pay taxes on it and eventually abandoned it.

They currently use it as a hunting cabin for when people come to town or the city officials just want to get away. Just recently they added a security system and update the interior, more for show than actual functionality. Never in a million years did they think that they would actually need to use it to keep someone safe. Luckily, most of the people that used the cabin didn't exactly brag about the little hideout so it wasn't something that a lot of people knew about.

When I first got the call, and we decided that the little cabin was our best option as a safe house I called my wife. She would know what was needed and had access to various resources through her charity work. I was expecting some clothes and some food but what she did was so much more than that. She wanted it to feel like a vacation, to keep Hannah and Quinn from feeling so out of their own comfort zone. Clothes and toys, a pantry and fridge full of food. I may be biased but I think my wife might just be the most amazing woman in the world.

As I enter my office I am stopped by my secretary,

she's on the phone but she hands me a bright pink post-it note that just says "Line 2". Who is calling on my business line? Anyone that I would need to talk to has my cell and knows they have a much better chance of reaching me on it. I hold my finger out to gesture to her that I would need another minute before I could take the call, they would need to wait. I have to update the room full of agents and marshals, this case is my one and only priority and whoever is on the phone will either accept that or call back when it's over.

"They should be arriving at the safe house soon. The officer escorting them will reach back out to me when he leaves the location." I call out from the doorway. Not everyone is paying attention, but the ones that need to be and the rest will be caught up when the time is ready.

"Jane, can you put in a pizza order for pick up. Do a couple of large pizzas. Whatever you think the girls would like." I say walking by my secretary's desk again.

As I sit down at my desk I pick up the old phone and press "Line 2".

"This is the chief," I say with a sigh.

The voice on the line doesn't identify himself but I know immediately who it is. Great, let's add one more thing into this already stressful day.

"Do what you have to do to take care of this. She's already been through so much." Is all I say before I slam the phone down.

Hannah

We drove for about twenty-five minutes, leaving Oak Bend fading away in the rearview mirror. I have driven these back roads hundreds of times before, but after the first couple of turns, I have no idea where we are. It seems like we are driving in circles, turning one way and then turning another. I understand why they are doing it, no one will be able to follow us this way. The thought sends a shiver down my back.

By the time the van slows down and turns into a driveway, we are in the middle of nowhere. I haven't seen another house for miles, we will be alone out here. I'm not sure that makes me feel any safer. As we drove up the short driveway I can't help but notice all the trees, the entire house is surrounded by them. We came to a clearing in the trees and the place that they called the safe house came into view for the first time.

It wasn't a house at all, it was a log cabin. If the circumstances were different I might actually find it beautiful. I wonder what they use it for when there isn't a fugitive on the loose. Does someone live here? Is it used for hunting? I didn't even know it was out here, I wonder how many people do.

The cabin isn't huge, just a single-story building, but it's plenty big for Quinn and I. The exterior is made of wood and appears to be kept up well enough by someone. There are two windows in the front, a large one I assume is in the main part of the house and a smaller one that is probably a bedroom. There isn't a door in the front at all, which I find odd, I am not sure I have ever seen a house without a door. Attached to the house is a double stall garage that looks as if it's just a tad bit smaller than the house itself.

The driver pulls the van into the garage and parks it beside a small black sedan that has dark tinted windows. There's someone else here? I turn to the agent questioningly but he isn't looking at me. He is texting someone, probably checking in. He doesn't seem concerned, so maybe I shouldn't be either.

I waited for the agent to get out of the van before I moved. I am not really sure what I am supposed to do. He came and opened the door for us and grabbed my coat and bag. As soon as we are out of the back and the door is closed the driver waves to us and leaves. The large garage door closes as he backs the van back down the narrow driveway.

Looking around for the first time I notice that the garage is actually pretty big, there's a small wooden tool bench on one wall and what looks like a mess of camping gear on the other. What stands out to me the most is that there are no windows. It's lit completely by the bright lights on the ceiling and seems unnatural, cold even. The other thing that stands out to me is that there are two doors on the back wall. They are identical, one on each side. Plain white thick doors, no windows and they each have a keypad next to them. They look just as cold as the rest of the garage, but secure.

"Should we see what the inside looks like?" Agent Holder asks as if he could hear my judgmental thoughts of where we were standing.

I can't help but blush a little bit, I know that he obviously couldn't read my thoughts but I really should stop being such a snot about this. I just smile and nod, I need to be grateful for this man, I know it's his job to be here but that doesn't mean he has to be this nice. He returns my smile and types a code into the keypad by one of the doors. A few seconds later we hear a loud beeping noise and the click of the door opening.

The interior of the house is not at all what I would have expected a hunting cabin to look like, it looks more like a nice family home with a strong female influence. As we walk into the living room I notice that it is very nicely furnished with a matching couch, loveseat, and reclining chair. There is a fairly large flat-screen TV on a big white wall and there are some interesting paintings on the other walls which are a dark gray color. The paintings are bright which looks nice against the otherwise neutral colors in the room. It definitely appears that a woman's touch had gone into decorating this place.

Next to the living room is a decent sized kitchen, with an island and a breakfast nook. The countertops are granite and the appliances are matte black which looks surprisingly nice against the otherwise white room. My kitchen at home is as basic as a kitchen can get, I feel there is no need for anything special because I hate cooking and I won't use it anyway. I hope this agent knows how to cook, I don't think Paul's Pizza delivers out here.

Maybe this won't be too bad, Quinn is already exploring bedrooms and appears to be dealing with the situation okay. I have to admit that I do feel a strange sense of peace out here in the middle of nowhere. I don't think anyone will be able to find us out here or even think about looking. I do feel a little uneasy leaving my own house, would Mark look for us there? If he goes into my home I will never feel comfortable there again and I really don't want to have to move because of him again.

"If we are still here tonight you guys can take first dibs on bedrooms and I will just take whichever one is left. They dropped off some clothes for you guys earlier just in case, I am hoping you won't need them but if you do hope they fit alright. Uh, there's food in the kitchen if you guys are hungry. Or you can just hang out. Just make yourself at home..." He's rambling.

"I am sure they'll be fine, Thank you, Agent Holder." I interrupt him just make him stop talking.

"Oh please, call me Declan."

His smile warms me, I probably will call him Declan, but I don't want to get too personal with him. He is here to do a job and I am here to stay alive. I don't want to be blurring any lines, and I have to keep reminding myself of that every time I look at him.

"Oh, okay. Declan."

The quiet in the room is getting awkward, I should find something to do with my time while I am here. I set my stuff down on the table and pick up the remote control for the TV. I'm strangely relieved to see the Netflix app come up on the screen in front of me. If I was home I would probably be watching an embarrassing amount of serial killer documentaries right now and that is exactly what I want to do here. As I am browsing through the selections I am suddenly aware of Declan in the room as well. My friends always joked with me that I was probably on an FBI watch list somewhere because I am so obsessed with true crime documentaries, he is probably going to think I am a psycho.

"Can I watch a movie in the bedroom?" Quinn comes running up to me talking a lot louder than necessary, like usual.

Of course, I am not going to say no to that, it's not that I don't want her in here I just don't want to watch cartoons and I know if she asked to watch them out here with me I would say yes. I push myself off of the couch and follow Quinn down the hallway.

The bedroom Quinn picked is nice, it has a full-sized bed with gray bedding, yellow walls and a TV on a small gray dresser. Yellow happens to be Quinn's favorite color so the selection doesn't surprise me. I use the remote to pick a preteen sitcom, something Quinn has probably seen a couple of hundred times already.

As I am leaving the room I take a moment to look

around a little bit more, I notice the closet door is propped open with a couple of boxes of toys. Inside the closet, there are more toys and some games. I can't really decide if the sight of them makes me happy or creeped out. Why are there toys here and who do they belong to? I shake the feeling and leave Quinn to watch her movie, leaving the door slightly ajar as I walk back into the hallway.

Declan is now sitting on the couch with the remote in his hand flipping through the movie selection, I watch him for a moment before continuing into the room. He doesn't seem very professional anymore, with his suit jacket off and his feet on the coffee table. He actually looks human for the first time since I have met him, not like a big strong superhero ready to save the day, but as a regular guy. He looks up when he sees me walk in and hands me the remote back.

"I see the selection hasn't gotten much better since the last time I looked, three years ago." He jokes.

He's not wrong, but I haven't really felt the need to go digging around in the selection that is offered, because I stick to the same things all the time. I smile at him as I turn on a cold case show. He will probably hate the show but he's a gentleman and pretends as he does. He looks at the tv then back at me, giving me a confused but kind of impressed look.

"Huh. Interesting." Is all he says before he turns back to the television and watches the show in front of him.

We are two episodes and three murders into the show and just getting passed the awkward silence when we hear a loud beep and the click of the door opening from the garage. We both look up to see Chief Duquette walk in with a couple of large pizza boxes. I didn't realize how hungry I was until I smell the pizza, but now suddenly I am starving. Quinn must be too because she suddenly comes running out of the bedroom screaming "Pizza!" The girl has a gift, she can smell pizza from a mile away.

We all gather around the island with plates and pizza and pretend for a moment that my world isn't crashing down around us outside. Honestly, I did momentarily forget about everything going on but not for long. As I picked up my second slice of pizza I look around and realize that this isn't normal. I can't just pretend that everything is okay. It all comes back to me, the escape, the police station, the secrets, and the pizza. I drop the slice onto my plate and quickly run to the bathroom with my hand over my mouth to stop myself from vomiting all over the floor.

I am literally sick to my stomach with the thoughts of that man out there somewhere, looking for me. As I sit in the bathroom, head in the toilet, I hear someone walk in behind me, great someone is watching me puke pizza out all over the bathroom. I am surprised when I feel a cold washcloth pressed against the back of my neck. It feels good, but I continue to heave into the toilet until there is nothing left to give.

I look up to see that it's Chief Duquette who's looking at me with sympathy from the doorway. I was half expecting to see Declan but I am relieved that he hadn't been the one to see and hear me throwing up. I have known the chief more than half of my life, and he probably knows more about me than almost anyone else in the world. He came to my rescue when I was covered in blood and has kept my secrets throughout the years, risking his job, and with current events, maybe even his life.

"Thank you, Chester, sorry about this. It's just hard to swallow it all."

He shakes his head with a shrug. I know it's his job, but I feel given our history that he is probably going a bit above and beyond for us. I wipe my mouth with some toilet paper and flush the toilet, closing the lid before leaning back to rest against the cool wall of the bathroom. I close my eyes and take in the cold air blowing from the nearby vent. When I open my eyes I notice the chief is still there and is just staring at me.

"I was hoping to speak with you alone, but this isn't quite what I had in mind." he kneels beside me before continuing. "

"Hannah, what happened that night in my car. The months afterward.."

"Hey." I reach out and squeeze his hand. "We promised to never talk about it again, we're not going to break that promise," I whisper.

He nods his head in silent understanding and stood up to leave me in the bathroom to clean myself up.

I stay in the bathroom a bit longer than I need to, honestly, I am too embarrassed to go back out there, but I know that I have too. So I fix my hair and gain my bearings before walking back into the kitchen. I sit back down next to Quinn and ask her how her pizza is. The big pizza sauce grin Quinn gives me makes me think that she is enjoying it. Across the table from us the chief sighs, looking at his phone. He glances up at Declan with concerning eyes and then back at his phone again.

"I better head back to the station, I'll keep you guys updated the best I can." The chief sighs again as he gets up patting me on the shoulder and then shakes Declan's hand thanking him for his assistance, and makes his way out the door.

I watch as Quinn and Declan finishing eating, not trusting myself to try and eat any more of the discarded slice of pizza on my plate. When Quinn finishes her last piece she excuses herself from the table and returns to her movie. As I begin to clear the table Declan's phone starts to ring and he takes the call while walking out of the room for some privacy. I can't help but wonder if it's work or personal. He is a good looking man, he probably as a girlfriend or two waiting for him somewhere. He walks back into the kitchen just as I am finishing throwing away the trash.

He picks up the leftover pizza and puts it in the massive fully stocked fridge, then turns and looks at me. It appears as if he wants to ask me something but is afraid to. He looks around the room for a few moments before making eye contact with me and begins to speak.

"Hannah, I know very little about you or the escaped prisoner. We got a call from the chief and hit the road, we got a little update during the drive but just on what's currently happening." He is stumbling over his words, which sounds strange coming from the normally confident agent.

"You want to know why a man escaped from prison to find me, right?" I ask, and I can't even hide the amusement in my tone.

I have only ever let a small number of details about my life throughout the years and I'm not really sure what the chief chose to share with the agents. Everyone seemed to have an opinion on what happened behind closed doors when I was growing up, but I wouldn't cooperate with the investigation into their suspicions so their opinions didn't matter in the end.

"Do you know what he's in prison for, or was in prison for, I guess?" I ask him.

The agent picks up his phone and starts scrolling through it, I'm not really sure what he's doing but I assume he has the file saved somewhere. I watch as his eyes scan over his phone a few times before he finally answers.

"He was convicted of murdering your mother, and eh..." he trails off looking at me questioningly, not able to finish the sentence, but we both knew where he's going with it.

I look at him comfortingly, as if he's the one that needs the comfort. I am used to people feeling sorry for me, but they usually need more details than just that. Details that had never been released, but somehow people knew.

"He was the monster under my bed growing up, one day the monster snapped."

We're both quiet for a moment, I look at Declan who's looking at the floor. I can hear Quinn laughing at something in the bedroom, it's a nice break from the tension. Declan finally looks up and sighs, as he looks at me his eyes give way into a pain that I can feel deep in my heart.

"Hannah, did he hurt you?" he finally asks.

"It took him years to kill my mother, but we were all dead inside years before that." I nod, wiping tears away from my eyes before continuing on.

There's a moment of silence that is quickly broken up by three knocks, a loud beep and the click of the door opening. I had to break eye contact with Declan to see who it was coming in the house, I'm not surprised to see Chief Duquette, but he isn't alone. A couple of uniformed officers followed him closely into the kitchen where we were standing. I can't stop myself from suspecting something bad has happened, I think if it was not serious, he would have just called.

"We just got word that there has been a police officer shot and killed on a secluded dirt road for about forty-five minutes from the prison. Shortly after that, dispatch received a call from a woman stating someone had shot and killed her husband in front of their young son. The address given was not far from where the officer had been shot." Chief Duquette quickly tells us.

He looks miserable, but this isn't his first time hearing the news. I can not imagine what he had felt when he first heard the news. Mark murdered a cop, and an innocent man in front of his son, It's really incomprehensible. That's more people that are dead because of me. A young boy will be forever changed and grow up with the scenes of his dad dying in front of him, just like I had with my mom.

"They were able to pull the dashcam from the officer's car and confirmed it was Mark that had shot him. The car he was driving was registered to a guard that worked at the prison. They figured Mark then left the stolen car near the farmhouse and killed the man to get another vehicle, which he has probably already left somewhere. He is being careful. Stupid, but careful."

"Upon finding out about the escape, the prison realized that the guard was absent as well, they thought it was suspicious given the events that had taken place. They sent officers to his home and located him there, deceased. He was murdered a few hours ago. There were letters and other evidence that indicates that he knew Mark was going to be there." The Chief explains professionally even though his eyes give him away, he's struggling with telling them this, understandingly.

"Jesus Christ. He was a part of the escape wasn't he?" Declan asks.

"That's what they believe, yes. We have no leads on where Mark went but the new murders change things drastically. He seems to have a plan. We don't know what it is, but this wasn't a last-minute decision to run away while he had the chance. We can assume he has other people assisting him. Places to hide, cars, money. We just don't know." He replies sounding defeated.

Turning his full attention to me, the chief continues "The one thing that you have to remember at this point is there is nothing that you could have done to save them. This is not your fault, Mark is a monster, he is the only one at fault here."

I honestly stopped processing the information when I heard that the guard had been found dead. Even if he had helped with the escape, that man was dead because Mark wanted to get to me.

People were dying because of me, again. I just can't handle this right now, it's too much. I am struggling to catch my breath and the room is starting to spin around me, it feels as out of control as everything else. I look over to see Declan reach out to grab me just as everything goes black.

2002

"Happy Birthday to you, Happy Birthday to you. Happy Birthday dear Hannah, Happy Birthday to you."

I'm surrounded by my friends, my mom, and my stepdad Mark, it's my twelfth birthday and it's been a perfect day. We went roller skating, ate pizza and now we are about to eat this beautiful ice cream cake that my mom had made just for the occasion. I couldn't ask for a better day.

As we eat our cake and ice cream, Mark stands up in front of all of my friends and I can tell he's about to say something embarrassing. I will him to sit down but my will is not enough and I watch in terror as he raises his glass of soda in my direction.

"I would just like to take this moment to tell Hannah how very proud I am of the incredible young lady she has become. Your mother and I love you very much and I look forward to watching you blossom."

Good Lord, he's so embarrassing. I feel my cheeks heat up and everyone is looking at me and clapping. You'd think I just graduated or got married or something, I turned twelve, it's not that big of a deal.

I shouldn't complain too much, up until recently I thought maybe my mom's husband resented me or even hated me for some reason. I always try my best to stay out of his way because he treats me like I'm a bother like I'm in the way of their happily ever after. Recently though, he started asking more about how I'm doing, what's going on at school and inviting my friends over to hang out around the pool in the backyard. It's like after seven years he just realized that he is supposed to be my dad.

After cake and ice cream we clean up and say goodbye to my friends. I'll be seeing them all at school tomorrow but it's always sad watching them all leave. We live in a small town and everyone knows everyone else so it's not unusual when I see Mark standing around talking to the other dads. I hope he's not saying anything stupid.

When we get home I excuse myself to my room, like usual, giving my mom and Mark some privacy and myself some much needed alone time. I turn my CD player on and my favorite band starts softly serenading me through the speakers. My friends make fun of me because I still listen to a boy band that was "so yesterday", but I can't help it, they're amazing.

As I'm getting ready for bed I hear the volume of the music turn down, which is surprising, someone is in my room with me. No one ever comes into my room, no one cares enough too. I turn around to see Mark standing just inside my doorway he has a picture of me and my dad in his hand.

I look at my desk where my CD player is sitting, right next to the empty space where the picture once sat. The desk looks empty even though it's full of other junk. The picture is such a staple to my room it makes everything look different with it out of place.

I remember the day the picture was taken so vividly, it was a warm spring day. The grass was green and the flowers were just blooming. It was my favorite time of the year. My dad's too. I was four and it was my last spring with my dad before he killed himself. We were hunting for eggs that the Easter bunny left for us, a week after Easter.

My mother had told me that the bunny was running late because he had so many eggs to hide and we were the last ones on his list. As I got older I realized that she had made that up because we couldn't afford to have all the Easter fun until payday, but it didn't matter, I had a great time.

I pull myself out of the memory and look up at Mark. He's looking at the picture of my dad and me, a smile on his face. I don't know why I always assume he hated my father just because he was married to my mom first, they were actually friends long before my parents had gotten married.

"I miss my friend Hannah. I'm sure you miss him too." He says quietly.

"Very much so." I agree.

He sets the picture down on my desk but lays it flat instead of the way it was when he found it. The action is unsettling for some reason like he doesn't want the man in the picture looking at him.

I watch as he walks towards me and sits down on my bed, I notice for the first time that he has a box in his other hand. A present. They've already gotten me a few presents, some new clothes, a couple of CDs and some fingernail polish. I wasn't expecting anything else.

"Hannah, come sit with me for a moment. I'd like to talk to you."

I'm not sure what this is all about but I'm curious about what's in the box so I go ahead and sit down across from him, leaving a foot or so of space between us.

"Hannah, I just want to let you know that even though your mother and I are married I am not looking to take the place of your dad. He'll always be your dad. I want you to think of me as a friend. We are friends aren't we?"

I nod my head because that's what he wants to hear. I don't think we are friends. I don't want to be friends with him.

"Good. I want us to be friends Hannah." He takes a long pause before continuing. "I got you this because you are such a big girl now."

He hands me the present. I'm not sure I want to open it anymore, but I do. Inside the box is a beautiful wooden musical jewelry box. I haven't ever seen anything so pretty in my life. It must have cost a lot of money.

"Open it." He urges.

I lift the heart engraved lid and jump a little when the box brings to play music to the tune of "You Are My Sunshine." It isn't a scary tune, I just wasn't expecting it. I'm thrown off by the choice of music that I don't see the locket inside right away. I almost didn't notice that Mark's hand has moved from my shoulder to my lower back. I do notice however that he has moved closer to me.

"You've become such a big girl Hannah. You know I love you, and when you're friends with someone you need to show them how much you love them. Do you love me, Hannah?"

I can't answer him. I don't know what's happening but it doesn't feel right. I don't like how close he is sitting by me, I don't like where his hand is and I really don't love him. I don't want him here, I want him to leave so I can go to bed. When I wake up I want this to have never have happened. I want him to go back to ignoring me.

I just want him to stop touching me.

Hannah

Opening my eyes I am panicked for a moment because I am unable to see anything. The light overhead is so bright and I have no idea where I am. When my eyes get used to the lighting I take a quick look around and realize that I am not in my childhood bedroom any longer. It takes me another moment to fully realize where I am and that I am safe. It was just a dream, a really bad dream.

"She's awake!! My mom's awake!" I hear Quinn call out before jumping onto the couch beside me.

Agent Ridley, Declan and officer Cleveland all come piling into the room, they look really concerned. How embarrassing. I wonder how long I have been out and what's happened in the meantime. I look up at the clock and I can't believe that it is after nine. Quinn should be getting ready for bed.

I assume since we are in this room that Mark is still out there and we are not going home tonight so I should find some pajamas for her and get her ready to sleep. I vaguely remember what the chief had told us but I try not to think about it too much because I have things I need to do and concentrating on the bad news will not help with that.

"Hey, Quinn, why don't you find something to wear for bedtime and get washed up. It's getting kind of late."

"Okay mom, as long as you are okay."

I nod and wrap Quinn in a big hug before sending her into the bedroom to do as she was told. Then I look at the group of men that are still staring at me and standing a little too close. I smile and give them a smile, hoping that they accept that as assurance that I am going to be fine. They all laugh, probably just now realizing how close they actually were to me.

"You gave us quite a scare there, the medic said you just needed some rest, and to make sure that you're eating." Officer Cleveland speaks first, sounding honestly concerned.

"Yeah, I've had an eventful day. I'm sorry. Quinn must have been terrified."

"She kept the rest of us from falling apart," Declan assured me with a wink. "We made sure she knew you were alright, she wasn't out here the whole time, the toys in the bedroom kept her occupied."

"Hannah, you are one of the strongest people I have met, but if it's not in your best interest then we can keep the details of the investigation at a need to know level. We don't need to tell you about the bad things. We can just let you know when it's over, and you can go home." He said it but doesn't sound really sincere.

I'm almost taken aback by that, I get why they are considering it, I did just literally blackout, but would they really keep the details of something this important from me? I'm honestly not sure, but I really don't want to find out either. No matter how much I don't want to know all the horrible things that man is doing out there, I really need to know.

"No, please tell me everything. I need to know, Declan, I need to feel like I have an ounce of control here, even though I know that I don't. Please don't handle me with kid gloves." I plead.

He slowly nods but looks conflicted. After a few moments, they start explaining to me what they had found out about the guard and the connections to Mark, but that they had no new information about where he could be. He literally could be anywhere. I can't stop myself from looking at the large window in front of me, which is luckily completely covered by large thick curtains. Is he out there? Just hiding in the trees waiting for the perfect moment to kill me, or worse.

Verifying that all the windows I am able to see are covered, I decided to get up and tuck Quinn in for the night. I can't help but laugh when I see my daughter in footy pajamas. She hasn't worn pajamas like that in years, and they make her look much younger than she actually is, but that is alright with me. If I could I would make Quinn stay little and innocent forever.

"Hopefully tomorrow we can go home, but tonight we get to stay here and it's kind of like a hotel. Isn't that right mom?" Quinn asks excitedly.

"Yes, it's kind of like a hotel. Now get some sleep, we'll see what tomorrow brings." I kiss my daughter goodnight.

I head back out to the living room to see that everyone else has left and Declan's watching some FBI show. I can't stop the crazy laugh before it leaves my mouth and I am almost embarrassed by how funny and ironic I find this. My big bad FBI agent who lives this life every day is sitting on the couch watching actors pretend to be him. In between fits of laughter, I see that Declan has turned his full attention to me, and seems amused by my reaction.

"The only thing realistic about shows like this is the fact that you never see the agents with real life. There isn't much time for things like that in our line of work, so we like to take advantage of what little we have by watching men pretend to be us on TV." he chuckles.

I plop down on the couch next to him, noticing for the first time how small the piece of furniture actually is. Trying to keep my attention to the tv show is harder than I had thought, I can't help but get sidetracked by the fact that there is real life, even better looking FBI agent less than two feet away from me. C'mon Hannah, get it together, he is here to do a job. No matter what happens he will be leaving when this case is closed. But when was the last time I felt this comfortable sitting next to man, let alone a man that I hardly knew? Never. That's when.

Declan's phone startled us both when it began to ring. The way my heart is beating out of my chest someone would have guessed it was a gunshot, not a cell phone. He turns to me and chuckles a little at our reaction before muting the TV and answering the phone.

"Holder. I was afraid of that. No, we will be fine here. Okay, bring donuts and Dr pepper." He smiles at me with a quick wink.

How did he know that I am a sucker for Dr. Pepper? What a creep. A thoughtful creep, but a creep all the same. I hate to know what my facial expression is when he finishes the call and tosses his phone back down on the coffee table in front of us. He looks at me and stifles a smile, and then proceeds to pretend like he doesn't notice the look on my face.

"They are calling it a night. The roadblocks are still active, and you will still have a full security team but they are sending the detectives home. The agents will go to a hotel for the night and they will all begin again in the morning. Officer Cleveland will be driving around the area tonight to keep an eye on things, the Oakbend PD is really great, we're lucky to be working so closely with them. Ridley was the one on the phone, he's bringing donuts tomorrow." he explains.

"And Dr. Pepper?" I confirm.

He nods and then can't contain his laughter any longer, which causes me to bust out in laughter too. Soon we are both laughing so hard that tears are rolling down our faces. It isn't even that funny, but with the tension broke I can't stop laughing. My sides hurt and I don't even care, it feels good.

After several minutes, I remember that Quinn is sleeping on the other side of a closed door, so I try to quiet down and use my hands to fan my tear-streaked face. Trying to tell Declan to quiet down as well. He takes the hint and proceeds to try and keep from laughing by turning the volume back up on the TV and avoid eye contact with me. Which I am grateful for, because I know if he looks at me I would laugh again.

When I am convinced that I am through laughing, I decide to take a look at the man next to me. He really is good looking, especially when he laughs. It is definitely a sound I could get used to. But I know that I won't. I wonder if the circumstances were different if I would consider actually dating a man like Declan. Strong and successful, but probably never home because he is on cases all the time.

I haven't done any serious dating, well ever. Living with my grandma and having a baby in high school made that kind of difficult. It didn't stop me from climbing into the back seats, or behind bleachers with different boys though. I didn't need, or really even care for the sexual contact, but I did enjoy pretending that they actually liked me. Maybe they did actually like me, but I would never give them a chance. One and done was good enough for me. With Declan though, I wouldn't mind more than once.

Realizing that that was completely inappropriate I feel my face heat up. Before Declan notices I decide I better get some rest, so I excuse myself for the night. I hope my normal nightmares are replaced with dreams of a certain good looking agent.

2003

Mark has been sneaking into my bedroom after my mother falls asleep for months now. I want to tell her, tell anyone but why would they believe me. Everyone loves Mark and he has done so much for us, my mother would never believe me, she would never leave him. So I just let him touch me in ways that I have never been touched before, I know that at my age no one should be touching me there.

We are sitting at the dinner table eating chicken and rice, I pass the green beans to Mark to hand to my mother on the other side of him. His fingers linger on mine just a moment longer than necessary and the smile on his face makes me sick. I look at my mother who has her eyes glued to our hands. She saw it too.

"What's going on? What is this Mark?" She asks, the shock easily detectable in her voice.

"What are you talking about? They're green beans." He plays it off, handing her the dish.

She doesn't take it, she just lets him hold it out to her for several minutes. She looks back and forth between us. I can't say anything, but tears fill my eyes, threatening to break free. I know this could go two ways. In my favor or not. I already know that it's not going to end the way I want. There is no right way.

"What are you trying to say?" Mark asks. His tone is threatening, I involuntarily shudder as the tension builds.

"Huh? Do you have something to say?" Suddenly the dish holding the green beans crashes against the wall beside my mother's head.

I push myself back to get away from the flying ceramic, my mother wasn't so lucky. Pieces of the sharp dish and green beans cover her face and upper body as she tries to shield herself from Mark's anger. The vegetables barely hit the carpet before Mark is up out of the chair pulling my mother out of hers as well.

I have never seen him react like this at any time, it just came out of nowhere. His anger pours out of him as he screams in my mother's face saying that she has no right to accuse him of anything, that she was nothing without him. I don't want to see this, I can't stop it so I run. I run out of the dining room and down the hallway. I know if I go to my room he will find me. So instead I slide into the closet shutting the door behind me.

The closet is deep, coats hang down in the front but there is storage space in the back. Just enough room for me to sit back here in the dark, hiding from what is happening out there. I have never seen Mark get violent with my mother before, to see that he has that control over her confirms my fears. She isn't going to stop him.

I wake up still hiding in the back of the closet, I don't know how long I have been here or why they haven't tried to find me. Maybe they have, but if I can hear them yelling at each other, I should be able to hear them call out for me. I open the door and see that it's dark out through the windows in the kitchen. The house is quiet, eerily quiet.

I tiptoe into my room, not wanting to wake anyone up. I don't turn on the light but I am half expecting to see Mark in my bed waiting for me. I am relieved to see that it is perfectly made just like I had left it this morning when I went to school. He's not here, he hasn't been here. The clock on my wall tells me it's a little after three in the morning, he isn't coming in tonight.

The realization should put me at ease, but I know that I am never safe from his greedy fingers, he will always be here. So I still lay awake all night, waiting to hear his footsteps in the hallway. They don't come, but shortly after six, I hear my mother come out of their bedroom and go into the bathroom.

I wait a moment to see if he will follow her before I climb out of bed and creep down the hallway to see her. She didn't shut the door all the way and from the crack in the door, I see her standing in front of the mirror. Her face is red and puffy, she looks like she hasn't gotten any sleep either, but that's not the worst of it. I can't look away from the black and blue bruises that cover her left eye and spreads down through her cheek. I allow my tears to fall as I lean against the wall watching her cover up the marks he left on her. Just like I cover up the invisible marks he leaves on me every night.

Chief Duquette

Sitting in my office has become my least favorite thing to do lately, it seems like every time I am in there it's because I have no leads and nothing else that I can do except wait. I have never been good at waiting. As the screen on my old computer comes to life, finally, I click to open my recent emails. I had asked my secretary to send me anything she could find on Hannah's, hopefully, ex-boyfriend Matthew. I don't know what it is about that guy, maybe it was the way he had acted at the station the other day or maybe it was just that I am a little too protective over the girls, but I don't like him. So a background check seemed like the best way to go about it. Hopefully, I will find something that I can run with.

When the background check comes in though, it, unfortunately, appears to be clean. Random traffic stops, speeding tickets, seat belt violations, but nothing that jumps out right away. As I continue to read though, I do find something interesting. Matthew Larson married Latisha Harring two years prior, there was no record of a divorce. It appeared that they were still married. That would explain why he didn't want to be a part of the investigation. There's a chance his wife might find out what he's been doing, or who.

According to the file, Matthew resided in Goldengate, a town a couple of hours away. I pick up the phone to make a courtesy call to the Goldengate Chief of police. I get his voicemail, it is really late, he probably is at home in his bed with his wife, where I wish I was right now. I left a voicemail requesting a callback at his earliest convenience and hang up the phone. As I did I heard the familiar chime of my cell phone. Reaching into my pocket I realize that it's not there. Damn it. Moving around the stacks of papers on my desk, I curse myself for allowing it to become such a mess.

Finally locating it under a paper bag leftover from dinner, I pick it up and see who's texting me this late. Cleveland, I don't know why my wife put all the officers in my phone by their last names, but it definitely makes it easier. "She's still safe." is all the text says. That's all that I need it to say, that's why I put my best officer as back up protection. Not that I don't trust the FBI, I just trust my own men more.

Jeff Cleveland has been an officer on the force for over five years, he is one of the main reasons that I had even considered the chief position. Although Jeff is a little older than my own children, he quickly became part of the family. The poor kid didn't have any family of his own around here to spend the holidays with and we had plenty of space in our hearts to let him in.

Last year Jeff arranged and hosted a fundraiser for a family that had suffered a devastating fire, with help from the rest of the police force and fireman it was a huge success. He went on after that to help with the rebuilding of the family's home. I had never been more proud of one of my men before, and I can't wait to endorse him for the chief position when the time comes. Officer Cleveland would make a great chief, and it would be perfect if he was credited with helping bring Mark down.

There's still no update on where Mark could be, they followed the bodies that he left behind him but the trail turned cold with the last one. There has been no sign of the stolen pickup truck and no new bodies reported. I hate to admit it but we would probably need to wait for the next body to turn up to get our next clue.

I sigh as I pick up a pile of papers, the transcripts from various interviews that were done in the last 24 hours. There has to be something here that gives some clue on what Mark is up to and where we can find him.

They interviewed a handful of prisoners who each had their own story, as long as they got something in return. None of which could give anything credible. The guards weren't much help either, except for confirming that the deceased guard and the prisoner spent a lot of time together and someone had messed with the cameras throughout two hallways in the prison.

I am glad that I had requested the Feds to come in and assist with the investigation, even though the DOC or US Marshals probably would have reached out to them anyway. I specifically asked my old friend for a security team to protect Hannah, he said he sent the best that he had. I hope that he's right, I am still nervous even though I know that she is tucked away where no one could be looking for her.

Looking through the files again I am frustrated with the little they had. The top set of documents was what information they had on Mark, most of it pulled from the murder investigation 11 years ago. There were all of the details of the crime, well what was disclosed at the trial and sentencing anyway.

I was just a patrolman when Hannah's mom was shot, I had just gotten off duty when the calls came in from a number of people reporting shots fired. We were all dispatched to the scene and it was one of the hardest crime scenes I had ever been to. There was so much blood, and then there was Hannah. She was the same age as my son but when I saw her standing there covered in blood she appeared so much younger but wise beyond her years.

I just couldn't stand seeing her standing there covered in blood in the same room as her mother's dead body, so I put her in the back of my car and drove her to the hospital. I knew that it was inappropriate taking the girl from the scene but she clearly needed to be seen by someone, she was laughing one moment and crying the next. I didn't know how much of the blood that covered her was hers and didn't want to risk something happening to the young girl.

Looking at the files again I come across the contact information for the other Patterson son and their dad. The dad had passed away a few months back from cancer if I remember correctly. Even in the man's last few months, he refused to admit what a monster his son really was. He left half of his estate to each one of the boys, upwards of a few hundred thousand each. Neither one of them deserved the money, and Mark probably used his share to fund his escape.

The only person who Mark would trust with his half of the estate would be his brother Ray. He didn't live around here but there is a file on him from the murder investigation. I pick up my phone again and send an email to Jane to have Ray Patterson's file brought up from the file room. The recent cases were all digital now but the older ones were still stored in filing cabinets in the basement of the police station. Some poor uni would need to go dig through them until he found Ray's. That won't happen until tomorrow though.

As I hang up the phone, there's a knock on the door, I look up to see the US Marshals that are assisting with the escape case. What are they even doing here this late? Do they have to take time to rest? I wave them in and tell them to take a seat. They had to be just as frustrated as I am with the lack of anything happening with this case. When they initially came to the station they acted all high and mighty, stating that the protective custody for Hannah wasn't necessary because they were going to apprehend their prisoner before he got anywhere. It's very clear now that that is not the case.

"We have been fielding calls all evening from people

who have claimed to see Mark all over the state. None of them have panned out. We need a couple of your men so we can start looking into abandoned properties in the county, they would be better at navigating these back roads than we are." One of the Marshals admits.

I had actually already considered the possibility that Mark might be hiding out in an abandoned house or farm and already had Jane run a report on any properties that may be included under that category, I should have it in the morning. I relay this information on to the marshals, not wanting to sound smug but making it clear that it's already being done. I have a suspicion that when this case ends it's not going to be because one of these overconfident assholes did anything to help, although they will probably get a majority of the credit.

The Marshals must understand how we feel about them now because they don't seem too bothered by the way that I am talking to them. They simply nod and thank me for our cooperation, and everything that we are doing to assist with the relocating of the prisoner.

They set down a file of lab reports that the state lab had returned. Unfortunately, it doesn't tell us much more than we already know, Mark's fingerprints are in the abandoned car, and in the dead guard's home and both the cop and the innocent bystander was shot and killed with the cops stolen 9mm service weapon. The evidence is piling up but isn't getting us anywhere.

The last few sheets of paper are different. They aren't lab reports or autopsy results, they are lists and photocopies of what look like letters. I look up at the marshals questioningly before returning my attention to the documents. The first page has a prison header on it, it appears to be a list of items found in Mark's cell after the escape. There isn't much, some books, a bible, some posters. Nothing of much interest, except for some copies of notebook paper that were listed as found under the mattress inside an old bible.

These pages, on the other hand, I find very interesting. Initially, they look like letters but looking closer I realize that they are journal entries, and based on what I remember I am certain that they are in Mark's handwriting. The first couple of pages are rambles of prison yard updates, an inmate did this or a guard did that. There are anger and pain in the words, he was clearly trying to get the frustration out.

The last few pages are different though, it was as if he was writing a letter to Hannah, one that she would never see.

My dearest Hannah, I need you to know how much I love you. There was so much that happened that allowed us to be a family. As you know I met your mother and father in high school, the three of us were good friends. At the time your mother and I were becoming close, we were falling in love. It didn't work out for us right away, but the summer after graduation when I was getting ready to move away for college she had come to me telling me that she had made a horrible mistake and had slept with your father after a night of drinking and was pregnant. She was so afraid, your father was leaving for college too and she would be all alone. I promised her that I would help her raise you, that she didn't have to be afraid. When your dad found out about the pregnancy his parents made him step up and demanded that they get married. They both agreed and married before you were born.

I didn't like it but I had made a promise to your mother that I would do anything for her. So when I returned from college after graduation I met back up with her, she seemed happy but your father just wasn't giving her his full attention. He was busy working and she had found out about an affair that he had had with a coworker. He got the girl I should have had in high school and he had a family with her. He should have been devoting his whole life to that, but he wasn't. I confronted him and he said I was acting crazy. He said that they were happily married and things couldn't have been better for you guys. He was lying. He always lied.

I was going to let it go when I got the call from your mother, she said she had pushed him too far during one of their fights and he had gone into the bedroom and put a gun to his head. He told her if she left him he would pull the trigger, she didn't try to stop him. She said that she had had enough and that she was going to leave and take you with her. That he would never see you again.

When she came to me that night you were crying and she was covered in blood. Your mother needed me then, she held onto me and never let me go. You initially hated me, you just missed your dad, you didn't know any better and I didn't know how to make you understand my love for you. As you got older, I could feel our love grow.

That's enough of that, there's a whole other page but just that much made me feel physically ill. I was not on the force when Hannah's dad committed suicide but I had read the file. According to the report, his wife and daughter were not home that night, they were out at dinner with a friend from high school. The report didn't state who they were with, it wasn't a criminal investigation and wasn't necessary, but I would bet a lot of money that they were with Mark that night. The gun that he used to kill himself was returned back to the family, a 9mm. The same kind of gun that was used to kill his wife, the gun was never recovered at the scene of the murder though, it just disappeared, I would bet just as much money that it was the same one though.

Saturday

Hannah

As I open my eyes I am surprised by the sun hitting my face. It's so bright I am temporarily blinded before I block the window with my hand so I can get a better look at where I am. I hear the sweet sound of my daughter as she comes bouncing into the room singing some made up songs about donuts. I roll over and look at the time, 7:05 am. I try to suppress a groan, I never enjoy being awake this early, especially not on a Saturday. Although this is not a normal Saturday, and given the subject of my daughter's new song, I assume the other agents have arrived with breakfast.

Rolling out of bed I walk over to the dresser in the corner, hoping that there are clothes in here that I can wear today. I am pleasantly surprised when I open one of the drawers and see a good variety of things to wear. I hope I don't need all of them but I do like that I have things to choose from. I wonder who they belong to. It's a little creepy now knowing where they came from.

Before I change my mind I pick out a t-shirt and a pair of jeans and quickly get dressed. Before joining the men out in the kitchen, I need to use the bathroom, so I sneak around the corner without anyone seeing me. I quick look in the mirror makes me remember that I don't have any makeup with me, great. There is probably a room full of very good looking men in suites out there and I look like a homeless person, but there is nothing I can do about it, so I might as well get it over with.

The agents all stop talking and look up as I walk into the room, which I find oddly satisfying. Declan stands up and opens the refrigerator door and grabs a soda as one of the other agents slide a box of donuts in my direction. I'm honestly surprised there are any left. Between the number of people in the room and the amount of chocolate that my daughter has on her face, I assume the box would have been empty.

I accept the caffeine without hesitation but pass on the donuts, I don't need a repeat of the pizza incident. I can't help but notice the facial expression I got from Declan, he seems to be disappointed in me. I anticipate him saying something, like that I should eat something but he doesn't, not yet anyway. Which makes me wonder when everyone is going to leave, and why there are so many people here? Maybe they have an update, or maybe they just really like donuts.

"You should eat. You're lucky there's any left with these guys around" Officer Cleveland takes the stool beside me.

"Why is everyone here? Did something happen?" I ask quietly trying not to disrupt anything that might be going on.

"I will update you later, they will be leaving soon," Declan explains, throwing a look at the officer as if to warn him not to say anything more as he walks away.

Officer Cleveland smiles and nods as he watches the agent walk away but as soon as he is out of earshot the officer turns to me with a new sense of seriousness.

"Hannah, the chief trusts me with all the details of this case, if you have any questions or need to talk you can call me. I'll be watching the area so I'll always be close by," he explains as he gets up and slides his card across the counter to me before walking away.

I know that the Chief has always trusted Officer Cleveland with the ins and outs of my case, and I know that he knows that I know. So I don't understand why he needed to make such a big show of telling me again. No matter what he knows I have never felt comfortable talking to him about it. I would rather call the Chief directly.

I'm still trying to comprehend the situation as the men say their goodbyes and leave. Pulling out the chair next to me Declan sits down with his mug of coffee. The smell of it pulls me out of my thoughts, I hate the smell of coffee. I don't even try to hide the disgusted look on my face as I raise my hand to cover my nose. Declan laughs and moves the coffee to the other side of the table.

Quinn comes running into the kitchen with a big box that is overflowing with games and puzzles. The box looks heavy and the sound it makes when she throws it down on the table confirms that it is.

"Can we please play a game, I need a break from the other toys." She begs, smiling and giving us the best version of the puppy dog eyes.

Declan laughs and looks over to me and shrugs. We dig through the box and pull out the game Candyland. Quinn loves Candyland, even though she is a little old for it. We play that first, three times. Of course, Quinn wins all three times. She always wins, which is probably why she loves the game so much.

We play the games most of the morning, which is a nice break from what is happening outside the locked door of the safe house. For a brief moment during a round of UNO I can't help but to look around and wonder if this is what normal people do, do they spend Saturdays playing board games around the dining room table? Of course, this is definitely not a normal Saturday, and this will never happen again, but I hope when we leave here I can start doing this with Quinn more often.

I look over at Declan who is pretending to look at Quinn's hand of cards, making her laugh in hysterics. It seems we are all having a great time, and again I can't help but imagine a life with Declan in it. What would it be like if he wasn't here just for the case, if he was here longer? If he stayed for me. I know I shouldn't think this way because it was never going to happen, but I can't help it. It feels nice.

Shortly after eleven, Declan loses another game of Uno and declares defeat. He actually declares that he is much too hungry to go on, but the message is the same. We work together to clean up the games and put the box back in the bedroom where Quinn had found it, promising to pull it out again if we have time. Quinn decides to play with some toys in her room while she waits for lunch.

"She's a great kid, you've done a great job with her. Does she know about her dad, I mean who he was and what had happened to him?" Declan asks when she leaves the room.

"Uh, no she never got to meet him. He wasn't really father material anyway, but he gave me that beautiful girl. She's really the best thing that has ever happened to me." I explain, trying not to get into it too much.

After a few awkward moments, he seems to accept that answer and we start discussing what would sound good for lunch. I'm surprised to find that I am actually kind of hungry, a lack of eating tends to make that happen. I'm really craving pasta, but I'd be happy with anything at this point. We settle on spaghetti. It was easy and Quinn loves spaghetti. Declan cooks while I watch. I hate cooking and seem to burn everything that I touch, so I keep a safe distance. From what I can see everything looks delicious, the food and the man in front of the stove.

We all ate at the table together, like a normal family. I don't even realize that I have a stupid grin on my face until I glance up and make eye contact with Declan. He smiles and just gives me a quick little wink like he knows what I'm thinking. My cheeks burn red with embarrassment but I don't really care, it feels nice sitting here with her daughter and Declan all together.

"Declan, do you have any kids?" Quinn peeps up with

a mouth full of spaghetti.

"Nope. It's just me, not even a dog. But Agent Ridley lives close to me, so it's kind of like having a pet." He chuckles, which sends both of us into a fit of giggles.

"I had a dog growing up though, my brother named him French Fries, because he was a french bulldog and my brother isn't very creative. I wouldn't eat fries for a year after getting the dog because I thought they were made from dogs named French Fries." He continued while Quinn was rolling with laughter.

Declan continues to talk about his dog and all the fun they had together while we finish eating. Of course, Quinn has to jump in and let him know that I won't let her have a dog and that he should tell me how much fun it would be to get one. He promises that he will try his best.

I love seeing them interact it makes my heart swell seeing how well Quinn has adjusted to him. I don't think I have ever seen her act this way around Matt. I know that she is becoming attached and it is going to be hard on them both when it came time for him to go. Maybe he would stay in touch, for Quinn's sake of course.

When the dishes are loaded into the dishwasher and everything is put away we both end up back on the couch, but neither of us moves to turn the TV back on. I really just want to keep Declan talking so I can learn more about him, and he doesn't seem to mind. Hopefully, he doesn't keep his promise to talk to me about the dog though, I'm not sure I can say no to them both.

"So you have a brother? Are you guys close?" I ask, hoping to get him to talk about his family more.

"Yeah, my older brother Peter. He lives down in Georgia, we talk often but not as much as we used to when I lived down there too. He's going through a rough time so I like to keep an eye on him though." He explains like it isn't that serious.

He goes on to talk about his mom and her loss to cancer, that his brother is taking it harder than he is. He talks about his dad leaving, that he is probably out there somewhere, but he doesn't care to find out. I listen intently, I love hearing him open up about his family, but I do feel bad for the man who comes across so strong but is dealing with his own loss at the same time.

I reach over and put my hand on his to give him a little reassurance and as I way to let him know that I am sorry for what he is going through, without having to actually say it. He doesn't move and allows my hand to sit in his. The contact feels nice, warm, natural. I had done it to comfort him but it doesn't take long for me to realize that is probably comforting me more.

"So tell me about you, Hannah. Not the case, not the past. Tell me what you want in life when this is all over." He asks me, his hand still wrapped with mine.

I don't really know what to say, my plans have always been doing what is best for Quinn, I haven't really thought about what I really want in life outside of that. So for the first time in a long time, I do think about it before answering.

"I think I want to go back to school. I didn't really think about college after high school, I knew I needed a job so I did what I had to do to take care of Quinn, but I think now that she is older I would like to do that now."

"That's great! What would you want to go to school for, anything specific?"

"I want to become a victim advocate. I would like to help people that have been through things to remind them that they will get through it. That life can still be great. I mean given where I am and why I am here, I should probably wait to see what the outcome is before putting that on my business card, but that's what I want to do."

I wait with anticipation to see what Declan is going to say, I have thought about going back to school before but thought it was too far fetched of an idea. Now that I said it out loud to someone else it still sounds kind of stupid. But Declan is smiling at me, probably trying to come up with a nice way to tell me how stupid it all sounds. I didn't realize I was holding my breath until he opens his mouth to speak.

"Wow. That sounds like an amazing idea. I know a few people that can help you decide where the best place to take classes and what classes would be best to take to get you where you want to be. Hannah, you are amazing. You would be so great at helping people like that."

I have to fight back the tears, I didn't think it was even that great of an idea until I heard him agree with me and now it's actually looking like a possibility. If I get out of this house alive I'm going to take him up on the offer to get some information from his friends.

We continue talking most of the afternoon until we both give in to our yawns and droopy eyelids and doze off into a peaceful nap. Our hands still touching, and my head on his shoulder.

2006

"Hannah? What's wrong?" Officer Duquette answers on the second ring, sleepiness distorting his voice.

Crap. I woke him up. I look at the clock and realize it's a little after two in the morning. I didn't know it was so late. I consider hanging up the phone and letting him go back to sleep but another shocking pain ripples through me and I let out a sob.

"Hannah, Where are you? What's wrong?" He's more awake now.

"It hurts Chester it hurts! I think it's time." I cry into the phone.

As the pain passes I feel stupid for calling him, but I always call him. He is my police officer, he will help me. He always helps me.

"Hannah, how long has it hurt Honey? How often? Is your grandma there? Let me talk to her." He rushes, out of breath now.

I ease my way down the hallway into my grandma's room holding onto the wall as I go just in case another shot of pain hits me on the way. When I reach the bed I shake her shoulder, sobs escaping with every motion. Just as she opens her eyes a stream of liquid hits the floor and I start to cry.

"Hannah are you there? Are you awake." A pleading voice comes from the phone.

Taking the phone from me my grandma answers for me. "Her water just broke Chester, I will take her to the hospital now."

I wonder how she knew it was him.

When we pull into the parking lot of Oakbend Hospital I see the familiar patrol car of my officer. He is waiting for us at the door. Through the pain radiating from my body, I muscle a smile when he asks me how I'm doing. I'm going to have a baby, I'm not okay.

After an hour of pushing with no real pain management, I find myself holding a six-pound eleven-ounce baby girl. I know just by looking at her that she is worth everything that I had gone through and everything going forward is going to be okay.

There's a soft knock on the door and I watch as Chester Duquette sheepishly walks into my hospital room. My grandma stands up to meet him and wraps him in a big hug. She's not very affectionate but it's different with Chester, He's family now.

"How's the little one doing?" He coos walking towards us with a bright pink bear in his hands.

I take the bear and cuddle it next to me on the bed. I know it's for the baby but she's too little so I will make sure to just keep it safe or her until she is old enough to love it as much as I do.

"Thanks, Chester. She will love it." I gush.

"I hope she does." He smiles. "Hannah, I just came from Miller's place. He said he'll come in and sign the paternity affidavit but he doesn't want to see the baby. He'll be turning himself in when he's done here."

Tears filled my eyes. It doesn't surprise me that he doesn't want to see her but I wish he would. Then he will be able to see why all of this is worth it. Miller's twenty-five years old so he will likely be serving some time in jail for this baby, I just wish he knew that she was worth it. Her perfect little fingers, her soft baby skin. The long tufts of black hair on her round little head, and when she opens her bright green eyes they light up the whole room. She's worth it.

Hannah

I open my eyes to see Declan had gotten up and is now on the phone. I reach up to wipe the hair away from my face and realize that I am covered in sweat. I am probably disgusting, and I definitely need to take a shower.

Declan speaks quietly, talking on the phone with an unknown person. He seems to be doing a whole lot of listening rather than talking. I notice that his shoulders are tensed, meaning that he probably doesn't like whatever he has just heard. I can't hear his response, but I assume he is expressing his dislike to whoever is on the other end of the line.

He hangs up the phone and turns around, he doesn't seem happy. Whatever was said on the other side of the line didn't seem to impress him at all. Looking up he sees me staring, he smiles in my direction.

"They caught a break, not a huge one, but it's getting things going. They found Mark's brother Ray and what he told them led the police to discover a bank account that was controlled by both men. They have a warrant to get the records of the account. With that, we will hopefully be able to find out where the money went and that trail might lead us to Mark."

I'm trying to take in all of the information, he has money, of course, he does. The new attorney, the appeals, now the escape. Apparently, his father left him the money when he died after all. I assumed that after learning his son was a monster that he would've written him out of the will. I was kind of hurt that he didn't, not that I'm honestly that surprised. His family let him become the monster that he is, it's only fair that they let him continue on after they're gone.

"They also got a list of things found in his cell, which they are reviewing and the chief will come to talk to us about it later."

After hearing what Declan has learned I felt a small sense of relief, maybe the bank account would lead them to Mark, but then again he is smart so maybe it wouldn't. I check on Quinn, who is still napping, and then decide to figure out what to have for supper. Maybe it would be the last meal we will be eating here.

When I came back into the room I notice what a mess it really is, so I begin picking up the pillows and blankets, trying to give the room a sense of organization. When I have finished folding the last one of my blankets I walk into the kitchen to look at the options for supper. Declan follows me in the room acting strange, like he has something to say, but won't just say it.

"This is going to sound weird, but it seemed like you were having a bad dream before my phone had woken you up. You were thrashing around and crying out. I was debating on waking you up but I wasn't sure if I should or not. What was that about?" he asks, trying to sound polite but coming across as really curious.

I stop what I'm doing and turned around to face him, I know I was sweating when I woke up but I didn't realize that it was obvious that I had been in the middle of a nightmare. Now the hot FBI agent in front of me wants to know what the dream was about. I have become really good at lying to people about my past, the lies just come naturally to me now, but with Declan it's different. For the first time, I actually want to tell someone the truth, so against my better judgment, I decided to just tell him about the dream.

"It was like a memory, but I'm not sure if it really happened. You know? It seemed so real like I can remember it, but maybe it was just a bad dream. He was trying to find me, I was hiding in the closet, just like I did that night like I did a lot, but he always found me."

"Hannah, what did he do to you?"

I look up at him, trying to decide if I should tell him or not, it isn't too late to change the subject. He doesn't know anything yet, but this could finally be the chance I have to tell someone for the first time in ten years. Can I trust him? Would it scare him away forever? Maybe telling him would be the best thing to do. Then he will understand that I'm damaged goods, and when this case is over we can make a clean break. With a deep sigh, I decide to go ahead and tell him.

"It started when I was about five when he moved in with us. At first, he did everything possible to buy my respect, then once he had it he stopped caring. I always felt like I was in the way. My mother was grieving the loss of my father and didn't want to upset him, so he got away with doing whatever he wanted. By the time I turned twelve he must have realized that I could be useful to him, in ways that a twelve-year-old should never be used. He started coming into my room at night. I won't go into details, but you can imagine."

Declan is trying but failing, to keep a neutral face. I can almost feel the hatred coming out of his body. His ears are beginning to turn red and he is clutching his fists like he really needs to hit something.

"It was shortly after that when he started to act differently towards me, he bought me flowers and took me out to eat all the time. He became obsessed with everything that I was doing. By then my mother started noticing, causing them to fight more often. She suspected something was happening and he hated that she was coming between what he thought we had." I continue.

"That's why he killed your mother?" Declan guesses.

I don't bother to respond, tears streaming down my

face as I look away. Deciding that the conversation is over, I turn back around and begin to take food out of the cupboard for supper.

While Declan cooks for us, I go in and wake Quinn up so that she can clean up before supper. I'm embarrassed that I had just gone and told Declan all of that, but I have bottled it up for so long it felt good to tell someone. At least now I will completely understand when he leaves at the end of the case and never looks back, anyone would do the same. That's why my secret could never get out.

While Quinn's in the shower and the food is in the oven, Chief Duquette walks in the door followed by Officer Cleveland. I knew he was going to stop by to talk to us but I still hate the feeling I get when he walks in and I don't know what he is going to say. He looks like he is struggling with whatever he is carrying inside him like it's all too heavy to carry. He needs to get it out, he needs to tell me something.

He looks at the file in his hand and asks me to take a seat. I look over at Declan who seems as confused as I am, why doesn't he know what this is about? That really worries me, what could possibly be going on that even the FBI doesn't know? I look back at the chief, wishing that he would just come out and say it. Quinn will be out of the shower and will join us soon, I assume that this is something that I don't want her to hear.

"Hannah, they found some papers in Mark's cell. I wanted to be the one to tell you this. We haven't confirmed anything but we have good reason to believe what is written here is true." He doesn't explain further, he just hands me the folder.

I reach out and take it from him, slowly opening it I notice there is one piece of paper in the folder. It looks like it has been photocopied a few times, it definitely is not the original document. It's black and white but someone has gone and highlighted a portion of it with a bright yellow highlighter. I look over at Declan who moves closer to read what is written on the paper that I have in my hands. He starts reading before I have enough courage to, after a few minutes Declan pushes himself up, clearly upset by what he has read. I finally bite the bullet and begin reading.

I have to read it twice to even understand what it says. When I finally grasp what the letter says an involuntary gasp escapes from my mouth. Why would Mark be so stupid and leave this in his cell knowing that he was going to escape and it would be found? I look up to see the chief and Declan watching me intently, waiting for me to react to what I had just read. That's when I realize that the reaction I am supposed to give is surprise, I should be shocked that my mom was there when my dad shot himself. Except I wasn't surprised, because I already knew.

I look at Chief Duquette and tell him how sorry I am, but it comes out barely a whisper, and a tear slips down my cheek. I don't want to cry anymore but I feel like this secret will be hard to explain, especially to the man who has never done anything to deserve my lies. I know that I should have told him way back when he asked if there was anything else that he should know about Mark and what he had done. He wouldn't have told anyone, he never told anyone anything else. I need to say something to make him believe that I wasn't sure about it, the truth is too much to deal with right now.

"Mark told me the same thing that he wrote here, I didn't know if it was true. I thought he was trying to scare me. He used to tell me to remind me that he was the only one I could trust, my mother was a liar. I am so sorry, I didn't know that he was telling me the truth."

I look at Declan and back at the chief, waiting for someone to say something. There's a long silence as I watch the confusion and the pain on the man's face, he was hurt that I didn't tell him, and I understand why he feels that way. He would be even more hurt if he knew the truth, that I was actually there when it happened. I kept that memory locked deep down in myself but it was there waiting to be released, I was only four but I remember it clear as day. I was so scared seeing my dad with a gun to his head but I was even more afraid of my mother who was taunting him to actually use it. I remember that the sound of the gunshot seemed just as loud as the sound of my mother's laughter afterward.

Another memory invades my thoughts, one that I've kept hidden even deeper. The memory of holding the blood-covered gun, the same gun that was used to kill both of my parents. I never told the cops that I picked up the gun, that my fingerprints were all over it. I pointed it at Mark's head and pulled the trigger multiple times, it was empty but I tried over and over again. It wasn't until I woke up in the hospital the next morning that I remembered what had happened to the gun, where it went before the police came storming in. Where I had hidden it in my shocked state.

The chief clears his throat bringing me back to reality, he sighs and leaves the room to talk to Declan in private, Officer Cleveland looks at me from across the room, he feels sorry for me but maybe he doesn't know how to show it. Quinn comes bouncing into the room and sits down on the couch next to me, and begins watching television.

"Is everything okay, did something happen?" She asks with her attention torn between what's on tv and what's happening in the room.

"Yeah, everything is fine. The chief just needed to talk to Declan then they will be going and we will eat some food." I lie.

I'm numb again, and I wonder if anything will ever make me feel again. Maybe I really am broken.

2007

"Hannah, I know you've been through so much and this is going to be hard for you. Just answer my questions honestly." The state's Attorney addresses me from the front of the courtroom.

It's day four of the trial, and this is my first time being allowed in the courtroom. The last three days I have been shut in a windowless room waiting for my turn to get in front of the jury and tell my side of what happened. I know what the state's attorney is going to ask, she's going to ask me what happened that night. I've told the story to so many people, and it's gotten easier every time. I can say it now without shaking, but I haven't had to tell it in front of him.

I can feel him staring at me and it makes my skin crawl. It's been over a year since he's touched me but it's like I can still feel his rough fingers on my skin. I shudder and fight off the urge to vomit and turn my attention back to the woman in front of me.

"Hannah, is the man who murdered your mother in the courtroom today?"

"Yes, he's there in the blue shirt." I briefly flash my eyes in his direction.

"Let the record show that the witness has positively identified the defendant." The state's Attorney says to the judge beside me.

"The record shall so reflect." The judge answers.

"Hannah, how do you know the defendant?"

"He was married to my mother." I squeak out. I should say that he was my stepfather, but we didn't really use that word around our house. He wasn't my stepfather, he was my "Friend".

"Hannah, can you give us some insight into what it was like to live with the defendant?"

I clear my throat and look around the room, glancing through the curious faces of the jury. The sickened faces of the people in the courtroom in front of me, my grandma's comforting smile. I already know what I'm going to say. I've had plenty of time to think about it, I've written it down more times than I can count. My therapist said it would help, but I don't think he meant it would help today. At any rate, I am prepared to say what needs to be said. I look back at the state's Attorney to answer her question.

"Living with him was like living in a war zone," I recall. "It was loud, destructive and dangerous. The rare moments of peace were just as terrifying as the full-blown battle, I seemed to find myself walking through life as if it were a minefield. I learned the hard way that if I took a wrong step I would have to face his rage. His words, they were like shrapnel, flying at my face in a seemingly endless onslaught of pain; but I knew that it could get worse. Much worse." Tears formed in my eyes recalling the memories.

"I know this is hard Hannah, but can you tell me what happened that night? When your mother was murdered?"

I clear my throat again and use the sleeve of my oversized sweater to wipe away the tears. Looking down at the sweater my mind wanders off to all of the things that have lead to me being here, wearing this hideous brown sweater. It's too big on me, but it hides the extra weight I have gained. It hides the stretch marks and the fact that my breasts are at least two cups bigger than they were several months ago. It hides the shame that comes along with the choices I made after that night that led me to be a teenage mother, sitting on the witness stand testifying here today.

"Hannah?"

"Sorry, what was the question again?" I shake my hands out, trying to shake all those thoughts away as well.

"That's okay. Tell us what happened the night your mother was murdered."

"That night he was not just throwing his fists around, he threw everything that he could get his hands on. Empty beer bottles smashed against the wall, the dinner plates from earlier in the evening crashed to the floor. He was loud enough to wake up the whole neighborhood, but I knew that no one would come."

"Were you in the same room where this was occurring?"

"No. I was hiding."

"Tell me about that, I imagine you were upset."

"Objection, leading the witness." The defense attorney calls out.

"Overruled, the witness may answer the question." The judge decides quickly.

"I'd learned long ago that crying was useless. The closet had become my safe place, hidden behind the heavy coats I could almost pretend the ugly words weren't coming from the man who was supposed to be my father, and the desperate cries for it to end weren't coming from my mother. In the light of the tiny enclosed space, I waited for them to stop. I prayed that that time would be the last time, but I did that every time." A tear slips out and trails down my cheek.

"Then suddenly, the yelling stopped. I remember my breath caught in my throat as I tried not to make a sound. See, usually, the fights ended with a slamming door, I thought I had missed it. I pushed the coats aside and waited for any indication that it wasn't safe yet and I should stay put. I hoped the fight was finally over, but I was cautious in case it wasn't."

"Understandable, what happened when you left the

closet, Hannah?" She presses on.

I draw a deep breath but it's suffocating, the air is thick with tension. I know I am talking too much, taking up too much time. They warned me about this during prep, but I can't help it, I don't want to get to the next part. I know I need to though, so I continue.

"I was hardly breathing the hallway air in before I heard the frantic whispers and deep sobs of my mother pleading with her husband and begging him to forgive her. I don't know what she was apologizing for, I don't think there was anything in particular that night."

"Objection, whatever the witness might have thought is speculation, your honor. I move for that to be struck from the record." The defense jumps in again.

"Sustained. The jury will disregard the speculation made by the witness. The state may continue." The judge rule in their favor.

"I know this is difficult Hannah, but I am not asking what you thought the fight was about, I am asking what you saw and heard. It's not easy to keep your personal thoughts out of this but I need you to do your best."

"They were barely making a sound at that point but the desperate fear in my mother's voice filled every inch of the house and pulled me closer even though every fiber of my being insisted I bury myself in the back of the closet once more. A pitiful whimper clawed at my heart from the other room; something made this battle different than the countless others that had come before it. Through the whispers and whimpers, a metallic click echoed down the hall. It took the soft cries and twisted them into a primal scream. Every hair on my body stood on end, every nerve ending seemed to fire at once telling me to run, but I couldn't."

"What did you do then Hannah?" She asked while putting a hand on the table in front of me, a comforting act I think.

"I pressed myself tightly against the wall to keep from

being seen, I crept down the hallway, attempting to get close enough to make sure my mother was okay." The tears are streaming now, I don't bother wiping them away. "I carefully peeked around the corner and saw that she was standing right there, her feet were all bloody, cut open from standing on broken glass. Her eyes locked onto mine for a split second but I didn't see him, he must have been standing further into the poorly lit room. Even though my mother's eyes begged me to get away, I readied myself for a fight. I couldn't take the hysterical cries anymore knowing my mother was just out of my reach. I counted to three, I was going to close the distance between us and face the monster hiding in the shadows." I paused.

"Objection, referring to my client as a monster is the witness's personal opinion and detrimental to my case. I move for it to be struck from the record." The defense attorney is on his feet now.

The Judge appears to be thinking about it for a few moments, then turns his attention to me. "You have been warned by the prosecutor to keep your testimony factual. Please keep that in mind. Defense objection is sustained, the jury is to ignore the comment on the defendant's personal character."

I took a long look at the jury again, they were all on the edge of their chairs. Staring at me with such interest in what I was saying, some of them with tears of their own. The room is quiet, they are waiting for me to continue on, I think at this point I could tell them anything and they would believe me. The events run through my head just as they happened that night.

One. My heart was threatening to burst from my chest.

Two. The panic coursing through my veins was making me nauseous

Three...

"Okay, I need you to tell us what happened next Hannah, please remember to try to stick to the facts."

"Peeling myself away from the wall, I turned the corner only to be stopped in my tracks with shock. The ringing in my ears made me wonder if I was about to pass out; that the pressure was too much. I thought that the panic rendered me temporarily deaf. In the fraction of a second that passed from the impossibly loud boom to the moment I realized that I could no longer see my mother standing in front of me; everything changed. Something warm and heavy splattered against my face, turning my clear vision murky red. I reached up with a shaking hand to wipe away the sticky wet substance that had at that point seeped into my eyes. Looking at my hand I realized what it was. Blood."

The courtroom inhaled all at once. Everyone had been holding their breath but were so shocked by the turn of events in my testimony they couldn't hide it. I had them wrapped up at the moment so I looked at the state's attorney who nodded at me to continue.

"Go on Hannah."

"My mind was cloudy, my ears ringing, and it felt as if the world had stopped turning completely. At first, I didn't understand what was happening, my mind couldn't comprehend the situation around me. It was as if everything was moving in slow motion. All I could focus on was the blood still smeared on my fingers, I could feel it drip down my cheeks like the tears that I had refused to shed for so long."

"Suddenly I felt myself being pushed backward. The force that moved me caused me to fall as I rounded the corner. In my panic, I noticed the closet door hanging slightly open; the warmth of the light spilling out a stark contrast to the darkness that clouded my vision. I longed for the safety I'd felt just moments before. Hearing sobs, I thought for a moment that I was crying, until I looked up and saw him on top of me, clinging to me. He was mumbling over and over again how sorry he was, how he had to do it, she didn't leave him a choice. I don't know who he was trying to convince."

"That sounds like a terrible ordeal that you had gone through, what happened next?" The state's attorney was drawn into the suspense as well, even though she knew it already. She had heard it before.

"The events had left me disoriented, at first I couldn't recall why I was lying in the hallway. My first instinct was to console the man desperately grasping onto me but as soon as I caught sight of the blood drying on my hands I remembered. The loud fighting and the piercing gunshot came back like a throat-punch and suddenly I was fighting for air."

"Why were you struggling for air? Was the defendant choking you?" The state's attorney cut in.

"Objection, your honor. Leading the witness. The prosecution already knows what happened, she's trying to make my client sound worse than he is." Back on his feet, the defense attorney is starting to get irritated.

"I apologize. I was merely trying to point out that the events had caused my witness a great deal of anxiety. I will rephrase the question."

"Sustained, please reword the question." The judge warned.

"Hannah, why were you struggling for air?"

"I struggled to push him away from me but his body on top of mine proved harder to shove away than I had thought. I felt my body react to the danger I was facing. This man had just shot my mother, this man was on top of me; as I struggled, I realized he had stopped crying. A strange calm seemed to have washed over him as he continued to hold me down. Pain and anger blossomed deep within me as I begged him to get off of me. I needed to check on my mother, I needed to get as far away from him as I could. Fear for the woman I loved more than anything gave me the strength to finally break free from his meaty hands."

I could feel a shift in the room, those who had been

just looking at me with concern and sympathy have now shifted their stares to Mark, no longer concerned but disgusted. The jury hated him too. I know that I need to keep the momentum going.

"Turning the corner, I moved slowly and cautiously, not trusting my own legs to get me where I wanted to go. I was shaking, but I'm not sure if it's from fear or something else. I looked around slowly, seeing blood everywhere, covering our new couch and the walls around me. I couldn't see where it had come from, it was just there, it was everywhere."

Remembering all of the blood throws me into a panic. I feel the pressure build-up in my chest and it feels like there is no room for my lungs to expand. I need air, water. I need this to be over. I start gasping for what little air I am able to get into my chest. I take a hold of the glass of water that I had been given when the questioning started and take a few small sips.

"Your honor, I would like to call a short recess so that my witness can get some air." The state's Attorney looks at me with concern.

No, I can't leave this room and come back in. I want to get it all done here and now. I take a couple more breaths and tell her that I am fine, that I want to go on.

"Okay, Hannah. Take another deep breath and a drink of water, then go ahead and tell me what happened next."

"Outside the house, the world was crashing down on us. There are sirens blaring in the night, the police were on their way. I remember being relieved as I realized someone finally decided to take action. One of our neighbors had finally had enough and took it upon themselves to alert the authorities to the horror unfolding within the walls of our home. Flashing blue and red lights had invaded the scene, illuminating the living room through the oversized picture window; illuminating the body lying at my feet."

The jury has turned their attention back to me. Soaking up every word that I am saying. I look over at Mark's table and see that the defense attorney doesn't look very happy. Mark though, as a smug smirk on his face. I want to slap it off, instead, I continue.

"I stared at my mother's lifeless body for what seemed like an eternity. I stared at the body that had been my mother only moments before. In the distance, between breaths, I saw myself cradled in my mother's arms as a toddler, helping bake cookies for the bake sale in second grade, shrinking down in the passenger seat as my mom hung my first bra out the car window when I was ten; a lifetime of memories cut short by a single bullet." Wiping the tears with my now soaked sleeve.

"Let's focus on what happened when the police arrived. Tell us about your first interactions with them."

"I didn't hear the door being kicked in or the sound of boots clomping down the hall. My eyes were still glued to the lifeless body in front of me. Faceless men in uniforms crowded around me, demanding to know if I was hurt. It didn't take them long to realize the blood wasn't mine."

"I had turned around to see that Mark had been tackled to the ground, an officer's knee pressed into his back, cuffing his hands. When the officer pulled him roughly to his feet, I notice he too was covered in blood."

In my head I go through the part of the story we decided to leave out, it may come up when the defense attorney questions me, but they decided that it may mess with my credibility, and with the jury eating the words right out of my hand I decide to follow directions, but it is still part of the story so say it, just not out loud.

Hysterical laughter suddenly erupted in the shell of the living room. All eyes were on me as I fought to contain the emotions swirling inside my chest. Every time I had prayed it would be the last time had led to this. I wanted it to end and it had; just not the way I had imagined. For the first time in years, tears streamed down my face as I continued to laugh; leaving bloody tears dripping onto my shirt.

At that point, the team of first responders probably thought I'd lost my mind. I heard one of the paramedics suggest that I was in shock and should be sedated, but one of the officers objected with the suggestion that they have me arrested too. My laughter seemed unending as one officer approached me. His kind eyes looked me over before instructing someone to bring me a blanket; I hadn't realized I was shivering, I hadn't realized I was barely dressed. He placed a gentle hand on my shoulder and told me everything would be alright as he led me to the back of a squad car and drove me to the hospital.

I can't say any of that but I need to end it somehow. My pause has extended too long. The state's attorney is going to step in again. She's going to see the panic in my eyes. I need to say something.

"Once he had been taken outside, an officer handed me a blanket and I was taken to the hospital."

"Thank you, Hannah. You are so brave." She smiled, I had done well.

I knew what was coming now, the defense gets to have their way with me. They get to try and pick apart my story, break down who I am as a person and make me out to be crazy in front of the jury. I know it's coming, but it's still a shock when the defense attorney asks.

"Hannah, what happened to the gun? You say Mr. Patterson shot your mother, then tackled you. Did he have the gun in the hallway?"

We both knew that he didn't, they never found the gun. That is a hole in the case, no gun. No time to hide the gun. Someone was shot, but there was no gun.

"I didn't see it. I don't know what happened to it."

"So you never actually saw my client with the gun, not after the murder and not before?"

"No. I heard the shot, I saw the blood, but I did not see the gun. I'm sorry."

"Hannah, how did you and Mark get along? Was he a good stepfather?"

I shudder. He wasn't, but I would never admit what he had done to me out loud. It ended the day my mother died. I would not let it come out to haunt me now. I blinked back tears and fought back the urge to vomit all over the smug man's expensive shoes. What does he know? What did Mark tell him? I look to Mark whose face has about the same amount of panic in it as mine does. I realize that he doesn't want me to answer either.

"Remember you are under oath, Hannah. You must answer my questions honestly and to the best of your ability."

I feel another round of tears breakthrough, I am about to answer his question when all of a sudden the courtroom erupts.

"I did it! I am guilty." Mark stands up and yells.

What just happened? What did he just say? Everything is moving so fast now, the judge is demanding silence and the people in the room are too surprised to give it to him. I look over at the state's Attorney and she seems just as shocked as I am. Did Mark just plead guilty to murder to stop me from telling everyone in this room that he molested me? Being a murderer is better in some way than being a child molester? It doesn't make sense. He has had plenty of chances in the last year to plead guilty, to admit what he had done, why now?

I don't get my answer though, the judge calls for a recess to give everyone time to work out what had just happened. I feel an officer pulling at my arm to remove me from the witness stand and I am met by officer Duquette who leads me out the door.

Hannah

After eating in awkward silence and cleaning up the dishes together, Declan suggests that we watch a movie before Quinn has to go to bed. I like that he is so good with Quinn, even though he probably thinks I'm a disgusting liar. I wouldn't blame him if he did, I think I'm disgusting too.

Quinn picks the movie, one that she has seen a hundred times before but if it makes her happy I am not going to complain. She seems to really enjoy it, but it isn't long before she's softly snoring on the couch between us. Her head drooping against my shoulder and drool seeping into the sleeve of my shirt. It's not very comfortable but I let her cuddle against me anyway.

The only thing that is keeping me awake is the thoughts that are invading my mind. I don't know what Declan thinks about me now that he knows some of the secrets but I can't stop thinking about how much fun we have been having in the short amount of time we've been together. I hope that for the rest of the time we are locked in this house it's not going to be awkward, but I imagine it is at least a little bit.

The movie never seems to end and after an hour or so I decide that I need to get up or I will fall asleep. I nudge Quinn awake and help her get up and go into the bedroom. She doesn't bother to change into pajamas before she crawls in bed exhausted. She's dealt with all of this so well, I am so proud of her. I just hope we can make it through this without her getting hurt. My sweet little girl doesn't need to grow up just yet. I kiss her soft cheek before walking out of the room, closing the door behind me.

Walking into my room I decide to go ahead and change into pajamas, well a long t-shirt with what I assume is maybe a baseball team logo on the front, and a pair of black shorts that are slightly too big but if I roll the waistband up a couple of times they won't fall off. It's closest to what I would normally wear and it's comfortable so I can't complain too much.

It takes a few minutes to change, but not as long as I had hoped. I'm really trying to put off going back out to Declan for a few minutes longer. The thoughts that fill my mind when he's around are completely inappropriate and definitely makes it hard to concentrate. Going into the bathroom I decided it wouldn't hurt to brush my hair for the first time today, and maybe even brush my teeth. Maybe there is some wishful thinking here, just in case Declan and I get a little closer I want to make sure I don't have dog breath.

Looking in the mirror, I realize just how much of a mess I really am. My face is pale and hollow, there are bags big enough for a five-day vacation under my eyes, and the messy bun I had earlier has all but exploded down the side of my head. I don't consider myself ugly but I sure need some help looking presentable today. Pulling my hair the rest of the way out of the bun, I run my fingers through it, scrunching it up to give the appearance that it was meant to look that way. I wash my face with a warm washcloth and brush my teeth.

Looking in the mirror again I decide I don't look that bad. Now I just need to prepare myself to go back out and see Declan. I stare at myself in the mirror for a few minutes, while giving myself a pep talk. I am a strong, attractive woman. If Declan doesn't make a move on me it's because he is too much of a gentleman. One last look in the mirror, I decide that it's now or never and walk out the door.

2007

In the months that followed the night my mother was murdered I had become increasingly close to the officer that had to lead me out of the house and taken care of me. He had become a very important person in my life. Too important maybe. Leading up to the trial I had tried spending every moment I could with him, even though he had told me on more than one occasion that I should be talking to someone else. Someone that could help me cope, he couldn't do that. But he could, he was my safe place.

Every nightmare, every bad day, every tear that I cried I turned to him to help me get through. Late-night phone calls became a normal occurrence and if I didn't see his squad car outside of the school every day I would throw myself into a panic attack. Every court date he was there, every time I was questioned he was there. He was always there.

When I had Quinn he cried. He vowed to me that he would do everything in his police powers to protect her as he had for me. The day he arrested the man on Quinn's birth certificate for statutory rape he proved that. We cried together that day. I think that was the turning point in our relationship. I knew that it had gotten out of hand, he was my hero but he first was a police officer that needed to do his job. I had to let him do his job.

That's when he brought in Officer Cleveland, he told me that Cleveland will be looking out for me because he doesn't have the personal connection to me that will prevent him from doing everything he needs to do to keep me safe. I didn't like it, but deep down I knew that it was what was for the best. I still craved Chester's attention, still wanted him near but when I looked out the window I saw Cleveland's car instead.

I was hoping that when the trial started I would get my Officer back, that he would stand by me during the process but he didn't. He kept his distance, it was for the best but it still sent me into a panic attack every time I had to think about doing it without him.

As he walks me out of the loud courtroom after Mark's outburst he keeps me at arm's length. I try talking to him, I need to know what this means. What is going to happen now, but it's too loud and he is too far away. He's just too far away.

He pushes open the first door that we come to out in the hallway and it appears to be an empty conference room. As soon as the door is closed behind us he wraps me in his arms.

"It's over Hannah."

That's all I needed to hear, it's finally over. I am ugly crying into his perfectly ironed uniform and I don't even care. It's been a long hard year and the secrets have eaten us both alive. All of the lies and the hiding have been so much to handle and now it's over. I can feel his body shaking with sobs as we hold each other, and somehow I know it'll be the last time. What we have is over, he no longer needs to protect me anymore. It's over.

Hannah

When I walk back into the room Declan has started a new movie, I don't even bother asking what it was. I just sit down and begin watching. The movie choice seems odd, from what I can tell it's about a little orphan girl. It's clearly a children's movie. Why are we watching it?

After a few minutes, I can almost feel the side of my face turning red as if someone's looking at me, I slowly turn my head in that direction. Declan doesn't even try to pretend that he isn't staring. I quickly look away and blushed even though I try so hard not to, given all the things I have told him this is humiliating. I wait a few seconds to build up my confidence, then I look at him again ready to confront him about making me feel like a freak. As I look, I notice that he is staring at with such intensity that I am actually taken aback for a moment.

The look that he's giving me makes me suddenly feel really warm, I can almost feel the heat radiating from my own skin. There's a static charge between the two of us that's almost unbearable, I can't look away, I can't move. I opened my mouth to say something but nothing came out. Declan's eyes shift to my open mouth and he slowly licks his lips, I close my mouth and look at him matching his intensity for a moment.

"Declan..." I am finally able to get it out but no louder than a whisper.

Saying his name sets him off, with a swift motion he has me pressed back against the couch, leaning over me so out faces are barely touching. I know he's holding back, trying not to cross the line, so I do it for him. I wrap my hands around his head and ran my fingers through his hair, pressing my lips hard against his. He parts his lips and kisses me back with a heated passion that I can feel through every inch of my body.

I've heard about people seeing fireworks while kissing someone, but I've never believed it was real, until this moment. The explosion I feel when we finally make contact is mind-blowing. I'm finding it hard to contain myself and Declan must feel the same way because his hands are everywhere. I try to match his passion as we explore every inch of each other's bodies.

Suddenly Declan stops and quickly stands up. He runs his fingers through his hair and walks around the small area in front of the couch before looking at me. An apologetic smile on his lips.

"I'm sorry. That was inappropriate. I shouldn't have done that. Even though I definitely wanted to, I can't."

I understand what he is saying, it is inappropriate, no matter how much I want his touch. I'm ashamed that I let it get that far, but I definitely don't regret it. Judging by how worked up Declan is he's probably regretting it a little bit. I watch as he goes into his bedroom and comes back out a few minutes later walking directly into the bathroom. It's not long after that I hear the shower running. He definitely seems to be regretting it at least a little bit.

I can't help but giggle a little bit, I hate that we didn't finish what we started but knowing I have that effect on him is kind of satisfying. I listen to the shower run for a few more minutes before heading off into my own room, it'll probably be less awkward if I wasn't still sitting there when he comes back out.

Sunday

Hannah

I smile as I open my eyes, I know exactly where I am, for the first time in days, I didn't have a nightmare. I had a happy dream, a dream that starred a certain good looking agent, and that is something that I can get used to.

I stretch my arms and legs out and look over to see that at some point Quinn had crawled into bed with me. I watch her sleep for a few minutes, this is so peaceful, I'm not sure I ever want to go back to the real world. I'm just thinking about getting out of bed when I smell bacon. Declan must have gotten up and started breakfast already. That is definitely something that I could get used to.

I carefully roll out of bed trying not to wake my sleeping child, and slip out of the room. I was right, Declan is in the kitchen still in pajama pants and a grey t-shirt that has "FBI" written across the front. He's busy flipping pancakes and tending to the eggs and bacon so he doesn't seem to notice me gawking at him from across the room.

He looks like he knows what he's doing in the kitchen, and actually looks like he's enjoying himself there. I watch him with a smile, I wonder what it would be like to have someone like Declan in my life all the time. It makes me almost want to stay in the safe house forever. Things outside may be crazy but inside they were perfect.

Declan looks up and gives me a very handsome good morning smile while inviting me to sit down and eat some breakfast. I don't have to be asked twice, everything looks and smells so good. I sit down on the stool across from where Declan is flipping the last of the pancakes. He hands me a plate that's overflowing with food, there's no way I am going to be able to eat it all but I will really try.

Declan finishes what he's doing and grabs a plate for himself before coming over and sitting beside me. We eat in silence for a few minutes before Declan turns and looks at me, his insistence causes me to stop chewing and put my fork down.

"I'm sorry about last night." He pauses and chuckles before continuing. "Not for kissing you, I am not sorry for that, but I am sorry for not being able to contain myself until after this was all over. I'll try and do that from now on."

I stare at him for a few seconds before busting out laughing. I can't believe that he just apologized for his lack of self-control when I practically jumped on top of him. I didn't miss the part when he said he would try to contain himself until this was over. So he has thought about what would happen when this was done and over with. I'm not the only one.

We are still laughing when Quinn comes out of the bedroom rubbing the tired out of her eyes. I wrap her in a hug and tell her good morning as Declan gets a plate ready for her.

"Can we go outside today. Please, I'm tired of being inside all day. I need sunlight to grow." She aims her pout at Declan.

He looks conflicted. Like he doesn't want to say no but he doesn't want to put them in danger either. He looks at me for help but I just shrug. I'd let him be the bad guy this time. But to my surprise, he says yes.

"Honestly, I don't think it would be a bad idea. But just for a little bit and you need to eat your breakfast first." He says smiling but I can hear the tension in his voice.

I want to object but I know that if he really thought it was a bad idea he wouldn't let us do it and I know Quinn can use some fresh air. I finish eating my bacon and leave the two of them to finish theirs while I go and get dressed.

I want to look nice but my options are limited. I decide on a flowy tank top and a pair of shorts, maybe I will get some sun while outside. I take a quick shower and brush my hair the best I can while it's wet. By the time I walk out of the bathroom, Declan and Quinn are both ready to go.

"I called Cleveland and had him to sweep through the area, he says all is clear so we're good. He will be driving around keeping an eye on things and will let me know if anything suspicious happens. We'll be fine." He smiles his most reassuring smile and adds a wink for good measure.

I don't even care anymore, I'm just excited to get outside and Quinn is practically bouncing up and down at the door waiting for Declan to unlock it. He slowly makes his way there taking his time as a way to tease Quinn and make her laugh. He pretends that he forgot what he was doing after bending down to tie his shoe, that was already tied.

We are all giggling by the time he actually gets the door open and we are finally able to get out into the garage. It looks the same as it had when we arrived as if no one has even been in there. Even though I know there has been a handful of agents and police officers in and out of the garage in the last couple of days.

As I had suspected the other door in the garage leads outside, into a beautiful backyard that led right into a wooded area. Quinn squeals as she runs outside and spots a tire swing hanging from a nearby tree. She climbs into the tire and begs Declan to come to push her. Calling out his name and giving him the puppy dog eyes. He runs over and pushes her really high as she screams in delight. The sound of her laughter is like music to my ears, her innocence warms my heart.

I take a seat on the porch swing where I can watch them play. The whole backyard is covered by trees so my hope for the sun is out but the view is so beautiful I don't even mind. I could stay out here for hours.

Declan walks over and sits down next to me on the porch swing, breathing heavily. Apparently, children are exhausting, as if I didn't already know that. He clearly isn't used to being around kids very often but he's really good with them from what I've seen so far. I wonder if he ever wants kids of his own, I'd have to remember to ask him sometime. Maybe when this is all said and done and I get that kiss he wants to give me.

We sit together for a while, side by side watching Quinn have a great time. Declan squeezes my thigh and smiles before looking down at his phone. I can take a hint, we have to go inside soon. I don't want to but I know that it's for our protection. Just then his phone begins to ring, the screen lights up with Chief Duquette's name. He answers it, walking away from me. That annoys me a little bit, I hate that he is using kids gloves with me. I know that I had lost a little trust when they found out about my dad, but I thought he was still on my side.

When Declan comes back he seems annoyed but puts a big smile on his face to tell Quinn that it's time to go back inside. I can tell that she doesn't want to go inside but she doesn't put up much of a fight as we all make our way back into the house. Quinn announces that she is going to go playhouse for a little bit and sulks into the bedroom. Declan waits for her to shut the door before he speaks.

"Hannah, the chief is on his way. Um.. the Marshalls are coming too. I don't want to speculate but it doesn't sound like it's a good thing. Duquette didn't sound happy."

I have no idea what the marshals were coming to the safe house for, the way it sounded their sole purpose is to find Mark. He isn't there so why did they need to come here. I assume I will be finding out soon enough, but the way Declan is acting is starting to concern me. He looks really stressed out.

I don't have to wait long at all, we are barely settled in when the door flies open with the marshals leading the way. They look upset, angry really. The chief is right behind them, telling them to calm down. He tells them that he is sure there is an explanation for everything. Now I'm really concerned. Declan is too, or that's what I assume by how fast he jumps up between me and the marshals.

"What is this? What needs to be explained and why are you barging in here like we are hiding the fugitive?" He demands to know, not moving out of the way.

"Hannah, the mail records from the prison indicate outgoing mail to your address and incoming mail from your address. You've been in contact with Mark?" The chief asks calmly.

That is one thing I was not expecting to be asked about. I was kind of hoping they wouldn't ask actually. I hadn't had any contact with him recently, but I did before. I didn't know he was planning an escape though! I obviously didn't ask him and he didn't offer the information. I would have told someone if I knew, why would I put myself and Quinn through all of this if I could have avoided it.

"That's a yes, where are the letters? What did they say?" One of the marshals speaks up, clearly annoyed.

"I didn't keep them. I swear to god I didn't know about the escape. I wrote to him years ago. I just wanted some information, an apology. Something that I could use to forgive him. He didn't apologize. He didn't give me what I wanted. He just wrote about how much he hated it there. I told him to stop writing, that if he couldn't answer my questions I didn't want to hear from him anymore. That's it I swear!" I surprise myself with tears.

The marshals don't seem any happier with my

explanation but the chief looks relieved and Declan is still fuming about how they approached it, he probably isn't even listening to what I'm saying. I told them most of the truth, I left out some things but not anything that mattered. It isn't going to help their case, it wouldn't help find him.

"What are you hiding?" the marshal demands, not backing down.

"Hey! Back off. She had every right to write to the man who did her wrong looking for answers. Just because you guys can't do your damn job doesn't mean you get to pick on the victim." Declan is pissed.

I don't understand why they are attacking me. I haven't done anything wrong, have I? I actually just got rid of the letters a few days ago, to rid myself of the past, to move on. They didn't know that and I am not about to tell them or they will think I'm hiding something, something else.

"Chief, I suggest you talk to your victim and try and get some answers from her. Maybe she will actually tell the truth once in this investigation." The marshal yells as they stomp out the door.

Declan sighs as he walks over and shuts the door behind them. He turns and looks at me and then at the chief. I know that I have lost some of their trust already and I hope that this isn't going to turn him against me. I know that I have Declan on my side, he seems really angry by the way they treated me but the chief is hard to read.

"I don't know anything else I swear, I didn't say anything because there was nothing to say." I plead.

"I know Hannah, the prison monitors the mail. If there was anything in any of those letters they would have caught it first. Declan is right, they are just frustrated at themselves. I am sorry that happened." The chief sighs.

That makes me feel a little better, but I hate that I was having such a good day and just like that the reality of the situation comes back and hits me full force. This man keeps on ruining my life, why won't he just stop. I can't help but get overwhelmed with everything going on. I just want to go into the bedroom and cry it out, but I don't want Quinn to worry. I have to be strong, I just don't know how much longer I can be, how much longer I even want to be.

The chief reaches over and squeezes my shoulder and sighs before walking out the door. I don't want him to leave, but I am kind of glad he did. I just want to be alone but I want to know someone is there for me too.

"Hey, why don't you go take a bubble bath, I will get Quinn some lunch" Declan being the gentleman he is, offers.

I hadn't really thought about doing that but it does sound really relaxing. I can't decide if I want to just sit on the couch and cry or go ahead and take a bath and hopefully come out feeling better. I decide to go ahead with the bath and thank him before slowly getting up and going into the bathroom.

I turn the water on just a little too hot and pour some bubbles into the water as it fills the tub. I strip off my clothes and look at myself in the mirror, tracing my fingers across the faint scars on my legs. They are barely noticeable but I know where every single one of them is. I started cutting myself when I was thirteen. Mostly on my legs, sometimes on my side, but always places where no one else would see them. No one but Mark anyway. I'm not ashamed of them, but I don't want to explain to other people why I had done it.

The room is starting to fog up from the hot water and so I decide to go ahead and climb in, the water burning my skin, but it feels good. I sink into the water all the way up to my face. The warm water loosening my tight muscles, loosening my restraints and with that, I burst into tears.

When I'm done crying and the water begins to feel

cold against my skin I climb out of the tub and drain the water. Getting dressed feels like a chore and I know that the bath is exactly what I needed but I don't feel any better. I wipe the water from the mirror and take one last look at my refreshed face before walking out into the cool air again.

Declan and Quinn are eating sandwiches and chips at the table and they both look at me when I come into the room. Declan points at the plate between theirs which has a sandwich and my favorite chips on it. A dr pepper sitting there ready and waiting as well. I give them a smile as I take my seat.

"All clean mom?" My daughter asks with a big smile.

"Yup. All clean. Now I am starving."

We talk about how cool the backyard is while we snack on our lunch. Looking at the clock, I realize it's the middle of the afternoon, no wonder I'm hungry. Another day in captivity was almost over and it's now clear that they are nowhere near finding Mark. The thought exhausts me. It feels like all we have done this whole time is watch movies, sleep and eat. This is not the life I can live much longer, I'm going to gain a hundred pounds and soon I won't be able to get off the couch.

"Let's play another game," I say out loud as I get up and walk into the bedroom to get the box of games out.

No one objects so we spend the rest of the afternoon playing games.

Hannah

We play games for hours, laughing and telling stories. It's actually a great evening. We throw a couple of pizzas in the oven and finish off the chips that Declan had opened for lunch. By the time we pack up the last of the games, Quinn's so tired she can hardly carry herself into the bedroom. When she finally gets in the room she doesn't even change into pajamas just crawls right into bed and is out like a light.

I'm tired too, but not quite ready for bed yet. I need to talk to Declan to make sure that he knows that I'm not hiding anything else, well nothing that I'm going to tell him anyway. Some things need to be left unsaid. I hope he can understand that.

After I get Quinn settled in I go back out to help finish cleaning up the mess in the kitchen but Declan has it all cleaned up already. That man is something else. He's sitting on the couch waiting for me when I walk in. Just sitting down beside him sends a shiver up my spine as I remember the actions of the night before. It seems like such a long time ago now, but the feeling I get just sitting here brings it all back.

I take a deep breath and try to push back the feelings, Declan drew a line yesterday that he obviously doesn't want to cross, I need to be fair to him. I turn the tv on trying to avoid looking at him, but it isn't working. I turn and look at him anyway, and I'm surprised to see that he's already looking at me. A small grin is pulling at the side of his mouth. A shiver shoots through my body again, he isn't being very fair. I bite my bottom lip trying to suppress a smile of my own. Declan tilts his head back and covers his face with his hands making a loud groaning noise.

Now I know that he's struggling just as much as I am, the self-control is strong in this one though. Or so I thought. Suddenly I feel his hands on me, gently pulling me closer. I don't object to his persistence, instead, I climb willingly onto his lap. I run my hand down his face slowly, testing the limits. I lean in and place my lips on his kissing him slowly, softly, gently. He quickens the pace until the kiss turns sloppy and intense. The fireworks are still there, going off all around my head as Declan turns and lays me down on the couch.

He stands and reaches behind his back and pulls his shirt off, revealing well-defined abs covered in a light layer of sweat that makes him glisten in the light. I run my shaking hands over his abs and up over his chest, his body is amazing and I can't stop myself from touching it. I playfully ran my fingers through his hair while he kisses his way down my face and onto my neck.

He slides down and pulls the bottom of my shirt up to kiss my stomach, toying with the waistband of my shorts. I love the way his lips feel against my skin, I never want him to stop. He slowly pulls down the shorts exposing my black lacy panties, a low growl escapes his throat as he feels the lace with his finger but I can barely hear it over the roaring in my ears from my racing heart.

Declan stops and slowly makes his way back up to my face, kissing my body the whole way up. He stands up and carefully lifts me up and carries me into his bedroom kissing my neck the whole way, not bothering to stop and turn the light off as he walks by the switch. He forcefully pushes me up against the wall and continues kissing my neck and jawline. Using the wall to hold my weight, he lifts my shirt over my head so he can kiss further down my body as his hands cup my breasts.

He stops for a moment and looks deep into my eyes,

desire in his gaze, I know this is it. We have crossed a line. We can either stop now and pretend it never happened or we can continue and live with the regret tomorrow. I moan as he leans into me, I squeeze my legs around his hips and press my body against his, wrapping my fingers through his hair I pull my face closer to his until my mouth is touching his ear and I softly whispered: "Don't stop."

Declan pushes one hand through my hair and gently pulls on it, using his other hand to caress my breasts, while feverishly kissing my neck, my chest, and my face. I am typically concerned about a man taking so much control, I always thought it would bring back bad memories but right now I'm so turned on I can't imagine him stopping now. I never want this man to stop doing what he's doing right now.

We fall into his bed, still wrapped around each other. He loops a finger around each side of my panties and rips them down my slippery thighs, fast and hard. Surprisingly they are still in one piece as I move my leg to help him take them off. He tosses them onto the floor and stops to look at me, I can feel the burning desire in his eyes as he looks over my entire body, his eyes drooping while he licks his lips. When I can't take it anymore I reach up and pull him back down on top of me. I have never felt this intensity when with a man before, and I need more.

I'm suddenly grateful for letting my doctor talk me into birth control, I assume that they didn't stock the nightstand with condoms and there is no way I'm stopping now. There is no way I'm going to let him stop either.

Mark

It's been about 48 hours since I'd found the farmhouse, and now I'm getting antsy. I should have gotten the call from my friend by now. He's supposed to tell me where Hannah is. I hate that I have no way to contact this guy directly, he's using a burner phone, and calling his personal number would be too risky. He sent me a text from a blocked number yesterday telling me to stay hidden, that it was too risky to try and make a move. But that was forever ago, I hope that he isn't getting cold feet.

All I can think about is Hannah and how much I love her. I know she will be grateful for everything I've done for her, and she'll be so happy to see me. Everything that I had done that night was for her, I did everything for her. The police, lawyers, and the judge just couldn't see that. They didn't want to listen, and wouldn't let me explain. Just thinking about it now made me so mad, this could have all been avoided, I could have had all of these years with her if they would have just listened! Now I need to make up for lost time, I need Hannah.

I'm starting to lose it, I feel like an addict going through withdrawal. I'm nervous and sweating, pacing back and forth across the small farmhouse. I have to get it together, the call is going to come. In the meantime, I cannot draw unnecessary attention to myself or the farmhouse. If only the damn old lady had decent food in this house. The food I have been eating while I wait here has been worse than the food they served me for the last decade in prison. If I don't leave soon I might go crazy with starvation alone.

Finally, the burner phone rings in my hand. The caller ID comes up as "unknown", but it has to be my guy. I answer the call on the third ring but don't say hello. Both ends of the phone are silent for a few seconds then I hear a low muffled voice on the other end of the line.

"Don't say anything. There is a cabin off of Oak Bend Road, 12 miles south of your location. Yes, I know where you are. The FBI is on the scene, give me two hours and I will cut the power to the alarm system." The voice doesn't say anything more before ending the call.

I should have known the bastard would know exactly where I am. The man really is good at his job, fortunately for me, he uses his skills to help the bad guys more than he helps the good guys that he works for. Having a friend inside the Oak Bend police department sure does come in handy when you are a criminal, and Officer Jeff Cleveland was a great friend of mine.

I had originally come in contact with Officer Cleveland through another inmate. He told me that the officer had helped him out a couple of times and that he was in debt to the prisoner for not taking the cop down with him when he was eventually caught. He let me call in his favor to get to Hannah. Apparently, the officer is more than willing to help a man get the love of his life back because he has been more than helpful up to this point and he is about to make it really happen.

I know I should stay where I am, I need Cleveland's help to get into the safe house that they are keeping Hannah in, but I can't just sit here doing nothing knowing the love of my life is just twelve miles away. I have to try and see her. I'll just sit outside and wait for Cleveland, maybe I could get a glimpse of her through a window, or she will be outside and I can take her without any help from Cleveland. I have the gun if I get into any trouble, I mean I already shot a cop, I am going to Hell regardless.

I decide to take the old green beat-up farm truck

parked in the barn instead of the truck I had previously stolen, someone might be looking for that, but no will be looking for an old woman's farm truck. I drive most of the way, careful not to draw any attention to myself in case I meet another car on the way. As I approach the area that the house should be, I decided to leave the truck in a patch of trees and continue the rest of the way by foot. I walk for several minutes, questioning the information that I had received when I came upon a clearing with what looks like a small cabin in the middle of it.

Chief Duquette

Frustrated with the lack of progress being made in this case puts me on edge. We have innocent people being murdered, a dead cop and no leads as to where Mark is hiding out. I want this case over, I want Hannah and the secrets that we share safe and I want Mark dead. I feel like we are doing everything that we can and just aren't getting anywhere. It's like Mark is always two steps ahead of us.

Picking up my desk phone I dial the cell phone number to my number one officer. It goes straight to voicemail. That's odd, my officers know when they were on the clock they should be working this case, and never let calls go to voicemail. I pick up the phone again and ring the front desk. Dispatched confirms that Officer Cleveland is on duty. He had called in earlier stating he would be on a call regarding the Patterson case until further notice. They do not have a current location for him.

That confuses the shit out of me. Nothing new has come in recently on the case that I have been made aware of, what call could he be on? Maybe he has a lead that he has decided to follow, but he knows better than to have his phone off and not call in his location, especially on a case that was this important to me. I make the decision to access the GPS on Officer Cleveland's cruiser, to see where it was. We already have one dead cop and I don't need another one.

Something about the GPS is odd. He has driven to the same location, about twelve miles from where Hannah is being kept, several times in the last 24 hours. According to his GPS, he is heading that way now. I pick up my phone and try and call him again but it goes straight to voicemail again. I call the front desk and have them try and radio him. While I wait for them to let me know if the officer responds to the page I call another one of my officers and tell him to pull his cruiser around. We are going for a ride.

We are just pulling the squad car out of the station parking lot when dispatch gets back to me and lets me know that there is still no response from Officer Cleveland and the GPS has him at the same location he has frequented lately. It's an old farmhouse owned by a widowed old woman who doesn't have any close family, and no one is answering the home phone registered to her.

We can be there in ten minutes if I use the lights, so I flip them on and push the speed limit down the road. Officer Cleveland probably has a good reason to be at the farmhouse but I need to see it with my own eyes. Then the officer is going to be suspended without pay pending an investigation into whatever he's been up to that made him break protocol.

I think the reason I am so mad is that this man has been my number one, my go-to for years, I was hoping that Cleveland would take over as chief when I'm gone. Now there is no way I would allow that to happen, I can't trust the rest of the men on my force in the hands of a man that can't follow basic safety procedures.

Before I know it the car pushing 80 mph, flying down the old dirt road out of town. As much as I want to get there quickly I slow the car down, no need to get ourselves killed, I have to make sure my officer is alright.

As we pull into the driveway of the farmhouse we see the Oak Bend PD cruiser sitting outside. Officer Cleveland is definitely here, but why? We slowly get out of the car, as we do we hear loud crashes coming from inside, I radio for backup and point for the other officer to go around back. I take my handgun out of my holster and creep my way up to the front door. I try to look into the window by the door but I am unable to see anyone inside. I quietly try the door, which is unlocked and slowly open it forcing myself inside the house, gun drawn on anyone inside.

Moving from room to room I scope the place out, making sure there is no one else in the house, when I open the back bedroom I have to muffle a few swear words. Laying in bed is the body of who I assume is the homeowner. It appears someone had just tossed her onto the bed after killing her. Another body, and if he has to bet Mark had something to do with it, but I can't be sure since I know my own officer has been here too.

I hear another loud crash and it takes me a moment to locate where it's coming from and when I enter the room I make sure I do so gun first, pointing at the only person in the room, Officer Cleveland. He seems to be having some sort of mental break down. He's destroying everything in sight, throwing furniture, hitting walls. I keep my gun drawn and notice the other officer on the scene has made his way into the back of the house and is staring at the madness from another doorway into the room. I nod at him and tell him to keep his gun out and ready. We don't know Cleveland's state of mind right now.

I clear my throat loudly to get his attention, when that doesn't work I yell, "Officer Cleveland, let me see your hands!"

The crazed officer stops what he's doing but doesn't look up or raise his hands. He is breathing heavily, sobs escaping from his mouth, the strong officer that we once knew is losing it. After a moment he puts his hand on his gun holster, not turning around but he does speak.

"This wasn't supposed to happen this way, he promised no one would get hurt. He just needed help getting to the girl. I am sorry, no one was supposed to die!" He cries, clearly distraught.

"Who said that? Mark? You were helping Mark get to Hannah? Jeff, please take your hand off of your gun. We can talk about this, I believe that you never meant for anyone to die." I try to reason with him but fear it's wasting time that I don't have. Mark knows where Hannah is, I might be too late.

"I'm not one of the good guys Chief. I lost my way. The money they paid was better than the money from the city. I thought since I was donating some of the money to a charity that I wasn't doing anything wrong. At first, I just turned a blind eye and let people get away with things and they would compensate me for it. Then they started asking for favors, but no one ever got hurt. I got in too deep and I owed a favor to the wrong person. I had to help Mark, I didn't have a choice. It's too late now."

"This isn't your fault, you can help us now!" I again try to reason with my officer.

"No, it's too late. He's killed too many people, and if he gets his way tonight an agent and an innocent child will be dead any minute now." He sobs as he quickly pulls out his gun and puts it to his head.

For the first time in my career I hesitate, really I just freeze. I should try and stop the officer, but I know that it won't matter. He's going to die one way or the other. I could stop him right now and waste the time I have to save Hannah, or I can just hesitate and let it happen. So hesitate I do. The few seconds it takes Cleveland to pull the trigger seems to move in slow motion, the other officer lowers his gun in an understanding of what is about to happen. We are both out of the room before the body hits the ground.

The backup arrives just as we are running from the house. We tell them to call the coroner and radio in to dispatch that we need additional backup at the safe house, then we jump into the cruiser and speed down the gravel driveway. We drive up Oak Bend Road pushing the car to its limits. No lights or sirens, we don't want to spook him and make him do something that we all would regret.

Mark

It's starting to get dark which makes it easier to hide in the trees, not that I think anyone will be outside to see me, but I need to be careful just in case. I am able to position myself so that I can see the road to watch for Cleveland or anyone else that comes down it, and I can see the cabin. Most of the windows have curtains that prevent me from being able to see inside. The large window in front of the house is covered but I can tell the lights are on because I'm able to see it shining through the sides where the curtains meet the edges of the window.

There is a smaller window to the right that's not fully covered, the curtains have been opened as if someone had pulled them to the side to look out recently. The light is on but there isn't much to see. It looks like a small bedroom. From my position, I am able to see part of the bed and an ugly painting of butterflies hanging on the wall. I hope that it's the room Hannah is staying in, she used to love butterflies, maybe I can get a preview before I get the real thing.

After a while, I start to get antsy, I have been sitting here for a couple of hours and I'm suspecting that I will have to wait for Cleveland to show up before I get to see my girl. I look at the time on the phone again, why couldn't he show up early for once in his life. It won't be long now but the suspense is killing me, she is so close yet so far away. Maybe she is waiting for me to come and take her away, maybe if she knew I was here she would come out willingly, without any force.

Fantasies of my rescuing her from the house invade

my mind, but then something catches my eye, movement from the open window. There's MY Hannah with some man. He has her pressed against the wall, he's touching her. He can't touch her, she belongs to me! I don't want to watch this but I can't stop staring as the man's lips move over her body, his hands touching her in places that only I should be touching. I am going to lose it. This isn't right. It's not part of the plan.

As I turn around to look again, all I can see are their legs tangled up together on the bed. I watch as the man fucks my girl right in front of me, seeing Hannah naked though, for the first time in so many years, I can't look away. She must work out on a regular basis, her legs are defined and her ass is perfectly shaped. Even with another man's hands on her, I am still turned on.

I struggle to unzip my pants with shaking hands and begin rubbing myself, focusing on the body of the woman in front of me. Pretending it was me under her perfect body, looking up into those beautiful green eyes while touching her breasts with my hands and my mouth. Pulling that sexy black hair until she begs for more, calling out my name in pleasure. I imagine the way her voice sounds when she is turned on when she is so into the sex that she can't keep her eyes open, the way she would gasp and moan with desperation begging me to make her cum. Finally, the pleasure would become too much for her and she would collapse onto my chest, into my arms.

Getting myself off for the second time, I realize how pathetic I really am. I have to touch myself and that man gets to touch Hannah! I can't take it anymore. I am livid. I turn around, pushing against trees and kicking the ground. It isn't fair, she was supposed to be waiting for me, what was that man doing with my girl. I decide I can't wait. I will get myself into the house. I am going to put an end to this. I'm getting Hannah back right now.

I run towards the house, just being careful enough not

to set off any alarms or security lights that the yard may be equipped with. Looking around the outside of the house I spot the utility box on the side of the garage. Shit. There are wires everywhere. "Just cut the black wire" I mock. Which fucking black wire? I check the wires and try and remember what I used to know about electricity. The larger wires look like cables, not something that would be used for an alarm, but that still leaves a handful of smaller wires that could go to anything.

I look at the box again. All the wires are going in and out of the same place, except for one. There is one single wire on the other side that is coming from a different section of the box. Could that be the one? I don't have much to lose at this point, Cleveland clearly isn't coming. I take the knife out of my pocket and slice through the wire. I pause waiting for something to happen, expecting some sort of alarm to go off indicating an intrusion, but there's nothing. Just the birds chirp overhead.

I don't know if that wire unarmed the system but the only way to find out is to give it a try. I didn't see a door into the front of the house so there must be one around back. I walk around the side of the house and stop when I see a blue sweatshirt sitting on the bench beside the door. Could that belong to Hannah? I pick it up and press it to my face. Inhaling the scent of the shirt. It's not strong but there is a faint smell of Hannah there. It's intoxicating.

Setting the shirt back down I check the back door, it's locked. Of course, it is. I check the edge of the door to see what my options are to get through it. Clearly, they were counting on the alarm system to keep people out, the door is crap. I take the knife out and slide it down the edge until I hear it click as it interferes with the lock and the door pops open.

Hannah

I think I am truly happy for the first time in a long time, cuddled next to Declan is where I want to be for the rest of my life. We haven't talked about what will happen when Mark is found and his job here is done, he will need to go back home, we probably would keep in touch for a little bit but our busy schedules will eventually make us drift apart. So I try not to think about it, I decided that I would take advantage of the time that we have together right now.

After the insane sex, we just had I leave myself tangled up in his legs. My head is on his chest, listening to his heartbeat against my ear, he runs his fingers through my hair with a gentle touch, I have never felt from a man before. It's perfect. In the silence of the house we hear the faint sound of a phone ringing, Declan's phone, he must have left in the other room. As much as we don't want to we know that he has to get up and answer it. He is still on the job and it's probably important.

Declan gets up and quickly slides on a pair of flannel pajama pants, following him off the bed I slip on my black lacy panties and pick up one of Declan's t-shirts off of the floor to put on. It's a grey shirt that has FBI written across the back in large black letters. It's long enough to cover the lace but short enough that I still feel sexy wearing it. Declan looks back as he walks out of the room and seems to agree with me as he smiles and playfully growls.

"Come back to me when you're finished" I wink.

I sit back down to wait for him but after a few seconds the silence is filled with the undeniable sound of a gunshot, and it was close, definitely inside the house. My first instinct is to hide, the memories of the last time I heard a gunshot that close came flooding back. I instinctively touch my face, feeling for blood, it was like I can almost feel it again. I cry out in pain, the world crashing down around me again, then I remember Quinn. I have to get to Quinn, the gunshot would have woken her up, she must be terrified. Praying that the young girl stayed in the bedroom, I head for the door.

When I peek around the corner I see Declan laying on the floor, he's holding his side and there's blood pooling around his hands. He sees me and gives me a look that I know means that he wants me to stay in the room, to hide, but I can't. Mark's going to find Quinn, I can't let him hurt Quinn. Trying to catch my breath and regain my strength I close my eyes. When I open them I catch a glimpse of a monster. He is standing in the shadows of the kitchen. I can see the outline of the same face that still haunts my dreams, and just like in my dreams he has a gun.

I have two options, I can try and talk to him until I can get close enough to get the gun or another weapon that I could use against him, or I can tell him what he wants to hear, and leave with him to keep Quinn safe. Neither option sounds like a good one, and I have a feeling this is going to end badly no matter what.

I bend down to check on Declan, to make sure he is still breathing. He whispers something barely audible and I don't know if I heard him correctly, I want to ask him to repeat it but I don't get a chance before Mark sees me. It sends him into a rage, he grabs the dishes that are sitting on the counter and pushes them onto the floor causing ceramic pieces to scatter across the room.

"I will kill him right now if you don't get your whore hands off of him! Dammit, Hannah how could you do this to me! After everything I have done to get here, to come back to you! I find you in bed with this man, he doesn't know you as I do! I love you, I need you!" Mark yells, crying and angry.

I jump, his unexpected outburst scaring me. I pray again that Quinn remains in her room, she's probably so scared, I can't remember if there is a phone in that room or not. Would Quinn be brave enough to call 911? I can't risk thinking that she had if she didn't so I need to come up with something and fast. I stand up and raise my hands up to show Mark that I am not going to touch Declan again, that I am listening to him.

"Okay, there. See? I am not touching him, I am backing away from him, just please don't shoot anymore, it's scaring me. I didn't mean to hurt you, I didn't know you were here. I didn't know that you had found me." I try to reason with him, using the fact that he's scaring me to try and get him to put the gun down.

Mark seems to accept that I didn't know any better, he looks down at Declan with pure hatred but doesn't make a move to shoot him again. I slowly move away from Declan, trying to keep a good distance from Mark but get closer to the bedroom doors. I have no idea what I am going to do yet but I need to buy time. Trying to process what Declan tried to say to me I continue to inch my way around the room, Mark adjusting his position to follow me but never letting Declan out of his sight.

The couch? Is that what Declan had said. What does that even mean? What about the couch? He's bleeding pretty badly, maybe he's going into shock and doesn't know what he is saying. If he dies tonight because of me I will never forgive myself. I close my eyes trying to think harder, then I hear something. It wasn't loud, I barely heard it but it was there. I open my eyes to see if Mark had heard it too if he had he didn't show any indication of it. Then I hear it again, very quietly, whispers.

I try not to give him the impression that there is anything else going on, I act casual as I continued to think about Declan's words again, it had to mean something. The couch? It just didn't make sense. I glance at the couch, it looks the same as it did when Declan scooped me off of it earlier, our blankets are thrown across it and falling onto the floor. The floor, from where I am standing, I am able to see the butt end of Declan's service issued pistol peeking out from beside the couch. He must have put it there for easy access while we were watching the movie. The blankets are blocking it from Mark's view, I need to get closer to it if I have any chance of getting a chance to take a shot.

Another noise in the bedroom stops me cold in my tracks. Not so much the noise itself but the reaction Mark gives when he hears it. Shit. He heard it. I don't even have to look at him to tell, I can feel it in my bones.

Mark takes two large steps in my direction, moving so swiftly that he is behind me holding a gun to my head within seconds. I don't even have time to react.

"Don't make a sound and don't do anything stupid, okay sweetie?" He whispers in my ear.

His breath on my ear makes me stomach toss, fighting the urge to vomit sends tears to my eyes. Just the smell of his breath brings back so many unwanted memories. Terrible things from my past that I never wanted to relive come crashing through my mind when all I want to think about is Quinn and saving her life. I fought through the emotions and nodded my head.

I allow him to turn me around to face the bedroom door, the gun still pressed against my temple. He motions for me to open the door, but my hands are shaking so bad I'm not sure I can get them to cooperate. He pushes me towards the door with a little more force. I let out a sob, there's nothing else that I can do now. He knows someone is in there and he's going to find out who it is with or without me.

Chief Duquette

We hear the gunshot come from inside the house as soon as we arrive on the scene. I know instantly that Mark is inside and that someone has been shot. With the curtains closed there is no way to get a visual inside and backup is still several minutes out. I have to decide what to do next and I have very little time to do it. I take off running to the side of the house, trying to remember the floor plans and which rooms everyone had been sleeping in. There are two bedrooms on this side of the house, I peek in one and motion the officer behind me to carefully look into the other one.

The first bedroom is dark and empty, I can't see anything and it appears the door is closed, blocking me from seeing the main part of the house. I am preparing to slide open the window when the officer at the other window waves me over. I quietly run to join him at the second window, looking inside to see what is going on. With help from the nightlight by the bed I am able to see the edge of little Quinn sitting beside the bed, hiding from the closed door on the other side. She looks terrified sitting there, her legs pulled up to her chest with her arms wrapped around them tightly. There are silent tears streaming down her face.

I have to get in there and get Quinn out. I get real close to the other man's ear and whisper my plans to him. The officer nods and slowly and carefully presses upon the window pane. As it quietly opens, I try to get her attention, trying not to scare her and keep her from crying out. She must have caught a shadow move, she quickly turns and looks at the window, seeing me instantly. I press my finger to my mouth letting her know she has to be quiet as I climb through the window.

Crawling from the window to the bed I wrap Quinn into my arms and whisper reassuring words to her as I hold her tight. I glance back at the window and I am about to tell Quinn to go to the officer when I notice that Mark has stopped talking. It was too quiet, I don't move. Waiting a moment, trying to hear anything coming from the other side of the door. I hear footsteps near the door and I know that I have to get Quinn out the window before the door opens. Pushing her towards the window I stand just as the door flies open, Mark standing in the doorway with Hannah in front of him, a gun to her head.

There is no way to get Quinn to the window from this distance so I shove her behind me. I'm wearing a bulletproof vest, if I get shot I would be okay. I have to protect Quinn. Hannah will never forgive me if something happens to her daughter. I look up at Mark and realize that he has Hannah in the right place to make sure I won't take a shot at him. If I try shooting at him I will hit Hannah, and he knows that I won't risk that. So I put my hands up, letting Mark know that I'm not going for my gun.

"Take your gun and put it on the ground, then kick it under the bed. Do it now! " Mark shouts.

I do as I'm told, taking my service weapon and kicking it under the bed. I normally carry a smaller pistol in my ankle holster but I forgot to grab it in the rush to leave the station earlier. The thought pisses me off, after the big to-do about my officers not following the rules I failed to follow proper procedure tonight. "Okay, there. Just don't hurt Hannah. What do you want me to do?"

"Come out here. Slowly. Keep your hands in the air. Who's behind you? Why is there a kid here?"

I can sense Mark getting frustrated, his plan is not

going the way he wanted and he is starting to lose control. I slowly lean over to give Mark a small look at the child behind me but I don't say who it is or why she's there. I slowly walk forward with Quinn at my side, as we get closer to the doorway Mark backs up keeping Hannah close to him, the gun still pointed at her head.

I immediately scan the room looking for Declan, it doesn't take long for me to see the agent on the floor, blood pooling around him. Quinn must-see too because she begins to cry harder, pulling herself closer to my body for comfort. I don't know where Mark wants us to stand but I am torn between wanting to get close enough to Declan to see if he is still alive and wanting to keep Quinn as far away from him as possible just in case he isn't.

We are just inside the room when Mark pushes Hannah away from him and towards us. He no longer has his gun pointed directly at her but is waving it around between me and Hannah.

"Hannah darling, who is this child and why is she here?" Mark asks quietly, in a sickly sweet tone.

Hannah

My heart plunges, but no one answers the question. I watch as he scans the room and I let out a sob when his eyes land on Declan laying in a pool of his own blood. I can tell by the look on his face that it isn't good, there's too much blood. I got my FBI lover killed, this is all my fault.

As we all get back into the middle of the room Mark pushes me away from him towards the chief. I want nothing more than to wrap my arms around Quinn and protect her from the bad guy, but I don't keep my distance. I don't want Mark to know that she is mine, I don't want him to think I care about her at all.

"Hannah darling, who is this child and why is she here?" Mark asks again quietly, in a sickly sweet tone

I freeze. I knew this was coming but I don't want to answer him, I don't know how to answer him. I look at the chief who is till holding Quinn close to his back and then back at Mark. I see the chief nod out of the corner of my eye.

"She's the agent's daughter. She wasn't supposed to be here, she's just an innocent child, please let her go." The chief answers for me, sounding sincere.

I look at him and then at Quinn and begin nodding, agreeing with him but trying not to seem too anxious about it.

"Yes. Mark please she is just a baby! Let her go outside, she doesn't need to see this and she doesn't have anything to do with this."

He doesn't seem convinced, I don't know what he's thinking but he appears to be at least considering the idea. He looks at Hannah and then at the scared little girl that was still clinging to the chief's shirt.

"Fine! Just the girl, get out of here!" He yells at the little girl while pointing the gun at the door that leads to the garage.

The chief all but has to force Quinn out the door, whispering to her that there were officers out there and she will be safe. He has to push her out into the garage and slams the door closed behind her. I can still hear my daughter's cries fade away as she runs from the garage.

"Hannah we need to talk. This will be easier if we just get done with it. I wanted to wait, give you time to remember our love for one another but we are running out of time and we need to go."

"I will do whatever you want Mark, please just don't hurt anyone else. Let Declan and the chief go. I will stay with you, just please don't hurt them." I sob, losing the confidence I had before I realized that I will probably never see my daughter again.

He smiles and then begins to laugh as he looks down at Declan again. I hate to even consider what he's thinking about but I know that he is crazy and it can be just about anything at this point.

"Just don't hurt Declan." he mocks. "Declan hurt me! Don't you see that I watched from outside the window while he touched you, he touched what was mine! I should gut him right here in front of you to remind you who you belong to!"

"But I won't." He continues. " I worked too hard to make this reunion with you. Do you know how hard it is to get someone from within the Police Department to help a convicted murderer Hannah?"

The confusion on my face is obvious, I turn to look at the chief, it's his department. Does he know what he's talking about? It doesn't take long for me to realize that he isn't as shocked as I am.

"Ha! Don't act like you don't know Chester, you put

him in the position to help me. Officer Cleveland's your main man right? Wrong. He's my man. He has been for years. Just keep an eye on my girl here, with your blessing. I guess I should thank you." Mark laughs.

I'm sick. Officer Cleveland has been at my house. He has been here. He's been to Quinn's school. He has been everywhere I have been for the last 10 years and he's been reporting back to Mark? Mark has known everything I have been doing. I turn to gauge the chief's reaction and he looks like I feel. There's a green tinge to his skin and he looks like he is going to vomit all over the floor.

"Oh and Matthew? His dad said he would do anything that we wanted him to, he's such a good boy, isn't he Hannah?" He laughs, harshly. "I must say I wasn't very happy with the plan, using my cellmates stepson to gain your trust and get in your mind. I knew that would lead to him getting into your house and into your bed. That I wasn't happy with it all, but it needed to be done. I had to know the person that you are today Hannah. You aren't the same pretty little thing that I fell in love with. You are a strong woman, still pretty though." He says with glazed over eyes, looking me up and down.

Mark opens his mouth to say something else but stops and tilts his head as he squints his eyes to see something behind me.

I slowly turn around to see what he's staring at when the realization hits me. They had placed a picture of Quinn and me together on the table on the far side of the room, just like the one that we have at home. Mark sees the picture of Quinn and now he knows that we had lied to him. Another secret I have kept hidden for almost eleven years is about to come to light, and Mark is going to be extremely upset about it.

Mark stalks towards the table and grabs the picture with such force I'm afraid that he's going to rip it in half. He looks at me and then back at the photo. I can't stop the tears from falling from my eyes, I'm not ready for this. I look up at Mark and then at Declan. Neither one of them knows the secret that has been locked deep down inside me for so long.

"Put down the gun so we can talk" The chief tries negotiating with him.

"No! My gun stays right where it is!" He yells, then pauses before pleading with me. "You have a kid? She's definitely yours, I see that now, she looks just like you. How old is she? She looks about 10?"

The tears are streaming down my face now, the time has come. I look at the chief and nod, the secret he had helped me cover up ten years ago was about to come to light.

"Please let me sit down, I will tell you what you need to hear," I say through tear-filled eyes, slowly walking towards the couch careful not to turn my back to Mark.

His face is full of pain and betrayal. Knowing what I know now about the Cleveland and Matthew, I don't know why he doesn't know about Quinn already. I mean they never mentioned the child that was with me all the time? I don't have time to think about it now, I have to figure out a way to tell him myself.

"Mark. I don't know what to say, but I know that I have to say something." I pause sitting down at the very edge of the couch facing Mark.

"When you were arrested, I couldn't tell you. It was best for all of us. I know you understand that."

"What are you talking about?" He barely gets out.

"Mark. I was about 6 weeks pregnant that night. She's your baby." I finally said it out loud, for the first time in years. The secret that only a handful of carefully chosen people knew. The secret that I vowed to never tell.

Mark doesn't move, he just stares at me in disbelief. For a moment I think he might actually cry, but he doesn't even blink. The silence is unbearable, I need him to at least say something, anything. He could yell, or scream or even cry, anything would be better than the eerie silence he's giving me now. Finally, he lets out a sound that was part laugh part cry, it sounds like a wounded animal and maybe that's worse than the silence after all.

He looks at me, then the chief and down to the picture of the little girl in his hand, the little girl he just let walk out the door. I can see the pain and confusion on his face as he realizes what he had just done. He lowers the gun and gasps for air, throwing his arm over his face for just a moment before becoming increasingly serious. He looks at me with the same hate that I watched him give my mother plenty of times in the past, and raises the gun pointing it right at my head.

"It's not her fault, I made her lie!" The chief yells out, distracting him for just a split second.

That second is all I need to reach beside the couch and grab the gun, I raise it up, hands shaking. I don't have time to aim or pretend like I know what I am doing. I point it at Mark and with every ounce of energy and courage I have left I close my eyes and pull the trigger.

After a few seconds, my ears are ringing and I open my eyes, Mark is on the ground, blood pouring out of his chest. The picture from his hand has fallen to the ground a few feet away, the innocent face of my daughter is now covered in blood. I'm not sure where I had meant for the bullet to hit him but after seeing all of the blood I am sure that this is not what I had in mind.

I can't move, the gun just shakes in my hands and I don't know what to do with it or myself.

"Hannah, it's okay. Give me the gun." The chief slowly walks towards me.

He reaches up and takes the gun out of my hands, releasing the magazine and setting both parts down on the table. I watch as he steps around Mark's blood as it puddles around his unmoving body. He kicks the other gun away from Mark's hand and bends down to check for a pulse. He slowly shakes his head and that's what I know that I had just killed a man.

My hands fly to my face in shock, I can smell the gunpowder still fresh on my fingers. The smell of the powder and the blood in the air makes me want to puke, but the feeling only lasts a moment before I realize that Declan is still bleeding on the floor.

"I need EMTS here NOW! There's a federal agent down." The chief yells into the radio on his belt.

I quickly look down at Declan and see that the chief is already there, he has picked up a small blanket from the floor and is holding it to Declan's bare skin putting pressure on the wound to try and stop the bleeding.

"You need to hold on, help is right outside they'll be here any moment, you just have to hold on, they'll be here." He's begging.

I run over to join them just as officers bust through the back door. A little late I think to myself, but they are a welcome sight nonetheless because Declan needs help. I want to stay with him to make sure he's okay, but the EMTs need me to move so they can save his life. They work around me the best they can, but with the IVs and needing to stop the bleeding they plead with me to wait somewhere that's out of the way.

The chief is finally able to rip me away from Declan only by reminding me that we need to go check on Quinn. I know in my mind Quinn is safe so it didn't even occur to me right away that my daughter is probably terrified even though she got out of the house unharmed. I look at Declan again as they are putting him on the stretcher, he is in safe hands. They will take him to the hospital and he will be okay. That's what I have to believe because although I just met him, I am madly in love with the man.

As we are following the stretcher out the door one of the other officers in the room pulls the chief to the side to talk to him. I can't hear what they are saying but they are looking at the gun that Mark had, the gun that he had shot Declan with. The chief turns and looks at me, he doesn't seem very happy but after a second he smiles at me reassuringly before turning back to the officer again. After a few more minutes I watch as the men shake hands and the chief returns to my side.

"What was that about, is something wrong?"

"We'll talk on the way to the hospital, they took Quinn there but don't worry she's with Martha"

Martha is a godsend of a woman, she has been a nurse at the hospital for a few years but she also works at the school part-time. Quinn loves when she gets to see her during the day and was absolutely delighted when she gets the chance to go over to her house when I need someone to watch her. I'm grateful that she is the one with Quinn when I can't be, but I want to see my baby now.

We climb into the chief's vehicle about the same time the ambulance pulls away to take Declan to the hospital. Waiting for the ambulance to get down the road, the chief slowly makes his way out of the driveway through the slew of police cars. I notice that the chief is holding onto the steering wheel so tightly his knuckles are turning white, he must notice my staring, as he loosens his grip and shrugs.

He is silent throughout the entire ride, right up until we pull into the parking lot and he turns the car off.

"Hannah, the gun wasn't loaded. He used his last bullet on Declan. But we didn't know that. You still did nothing wrong. When we get inside we will both be questioned about tonight's events. You need to be honest with them."

I'm confused and I have so many questions. Were they sure there were no bullets? I was so scared, did my fear makes me do something that I shouldn't have done, like shoot an unarmed man? The chief doesn't give me the time to ask, he is already out of the vehicle and opening the door to the hospital.

Hannah

"Hannah, I know you've had a long night and I know you're worried about Agent Holder, but we have some questions that we have to ask you. I wish they could wait but when a firearm is discharged we need to find out everything that happened." Agent Ridley is the one talking but there are three other people in the room with us.

As soon as I got to the hospital the chief and I were separated into different rooms to be questioned. I put up a fight, I don't see why this has to be done right now. Although the agent had reassured me that Quinn is fine and Declan is in surgery it isn't enough. I need to hold Quinn in my arms and tell her how sorry I am for what she had to see and go through today. I need to see Declan, hear his breathing to know that he is alive. Instead, I am in a room with two agents, a police officer, and a US marshal, being questioned like I am criminal.

"Can we just get on with it then. I will answer any questions that you have, I will tell you everything that happened. Please just ask me the questions." Frustrated tears fall from my eyes.

"Okay, let's start from the beginning. Where were you when Mark gained access to the house?"

Shit. I need to tell the truth I know I do. I look down at the blood-stained shirt that I put on in Declan's room and the pair of scrub pants they had given me to wear when I got here. It might hurt Declan's career, but I need to tell them the truth.

"I was in the bedroom, with Declan." I look up to make

eye contact with him.

"Okay." He takes a moment to consider his next words. "So you were in the bedroom with Declan and then what happened?"

"His phone rang, from out in the other room. He left the bedroom to go answer it. He was only gone a few seconds when, when I heard the gunshot." I sob getting the last words out.

"Hannah, I'm sorry that you had to go through this tonight. I really am, this is not what we wanted." He put his hand on my shoulder. "What happened after you heard the gunshot?"

"I thought about Quinn, she was in the other bedroom and I knew I had to get to her. I looked out into the living room and I saw Declan on the floor, bleeding. He was looking at me, I knew that he didn't want me to come out of the bedroom. I knew Mark was out there but I didn't care. I needed to get to Quinn."

"I walked out into the room and saw Mark, in the kitchen. There was no way I could get to the other bedroom, so I decided that I needed to make sure that he didn't know she was in there."

"Okay, then how did she end up out of the house?" He asks, curious.

"There was a noise, I don't know what it was. Mark heard it too. He put the gun to my head and made me open the bedroom door. The chief was there with Quinn, I don't know why or how he was there." I said, really thinking about it now that I said it out loud. "Mark uh, made him throw his gun under the bed, and then took us all back out into the living room."

"We talked him into letting Quinn go. He let her go." Even saying it out loud, it was still unbelievable.

"Okay, so he let Quinn go. Then what happened."

"I was able to make my way to the couch, slowly. Where Declan's gun was sitting. Mark didn't know it was there, the chief didn't know it was there. I did though.

Mark had the gun pointed right at me, the chief was able to distract him for just a moment and I grabbed the gun and shot. I shot him." Realization hitting me again. "Oh my god. I shot him." The agent held me in his arms as sobs riddled my body.

"We have more questions." The US Marshal stands up this time.

"I've told you everything that I know." I pleaded. "I don't know what else you want from me!"

"I want the truth, Hannah!" The large US Marshall yelled while slamming his fist down on the table in front of us, making me nearly jump out of my chair.

"Hey!" Agent Ridley jumps in "That's not necessary, calm yourself down, marshal."

I am grateful that he came to my defense but I know it won't matter. He can't make the man back down, we're passed that now.

"Hannah, I am not trying to make this hard for you, but I need answers. Your tears might work on the agents but they won't close this case. I will. In order for me to do that though I need you to tell me what you know. I need you to tell me what happened tonight. People are dead Hannah. We need to know why." He says sitting back down in the chair in front of me.

We've been going through this for hours. I have told him everything that I know, every little thing that led us to where we are now. I look down at the dried blood on my shirt. On Declan's shirt. I wish I could change what happened, there are so many things that I would do differently, but I can't. What's done is done, and nothing will ever be the same.

I can't help it as the tears fill my eyes again. How are their any tears left to fall? I wipe my face with my once blood-covered hands, I don't know what happened to the blood, but I imagine after the number of times I wiped away the tears I have some smeared across my face.

I don't want to cry, not in front of the Marshall. I don't

want to seem weaker than I already am, but I don't have the strength to fight it anymore.

"Hannah, do you honestly think that we believe that you didn't know the inmate was planning to escape? You haven't been completely honest with us throughout this entire investigation. We need you to start being honest with us now." He doesn't hide the annoyance in his voice as he sighs.

"I am being honest! I had no idea he was planning this! Don't you think I would've done something to stop him?! I would've stopped him. I would've." I'm not sure who I am trying to convince, I would've stopped him from escaping, wouldn't I?

"Would you have though? Maybe this was your plan all along. Maybe this is what you wanted." He sneers.

"How was she supposed to know any of this would happen? Everything that has occurred since the bureau took over has been out of her hands." Ridley reminds him calmly.

He was right, but the marshal isn't listening to reason. He is pissed that this case didn't end the way that will give him praise, or a bonus or whatever it is that he is looking for. They messed up and he will make it anyone and everyone's fault but his own.

"Let's try it another way, shall we. Tell me everything that happened, starting the day of the escape."

I have told them everything already, but I just want this done and over with so I take a deep breath and recall the memories from just a few days ago.

Monday

Hannah

Sitting in the cold empty waiting room is nerve-wracking, to say the least. Quinn's asleep down the hall in an empty hospital room, they had examined her when they brought her in, and a close family friend is sitting with her in case she wakes up. I told them that I refuse to leave the waiting room until Declan wakes up from surgery, so here I sit as the sun rises outside the window.

I think back to the last time I was sitting in this exact same waiting room, it was the summer that Quinn turned five. Little five-year-old Quinn was down the street at the neighbor's house, they had just gotten a new trampoline. Quinn was so excited when they invited her over to play with them. I, on the other hand, was not that excited and I knew one of those kids were going to be going to the ER by the end of the day, I just didn't think it was going to be mine. Quinn was on the trampoline for no more than three minutes when she bounced right off the side. After two hours in the waiting room, they cast her arm up and sent us home.

It won't be that easy for Declan though, the first couple of hours were critical for him, during which time I was being questioned by the FBI. The procedure they said because I pulled the trigger. After hours of answering the same questions over and over again, they finally seemed to be satisfied with my account of the events and allowed me to come to wait in the waiting room where I had learned that they had taken Declan into surgery. They won't tell me anything else.

Chief Duquette walks in with a cup of coffee in one

hand and a soda in the other. He hands me the soda and sits in the empty seat next to me. I open the bottle and take a small drink, my stomach is still turning after the recent events I have endured so I don't want to press my luck too much. I feel like I should eat something but every time I think about food I feel like I am going to be sick.

I look over at the chief and wonder if he had just come from being questioned too. I wonder what he told the agents, if he had continued to keep our secrets or if he figured it was over. I debated on telling the whole truth when they had asked me what happened leading up to the shooting, but I decided not to. If he did, I wouldn't blame him. It's hard keeping the secret after all of these years, I just can't put that burden on him anymore, especially after everything that has happened.

I just keep staring at the clock watching as the hands slowly move, one second at a time, listening to the ticks over and over again. I feel the man next to me shift in his chair, it gets my attention and makes me look away from the clock long enough to notice that the doctor has walked into the waiting room. We both stand as he walks slowly towards us, maybe he isn't actually walking slowly and I'm just losing it.

"Please sit. Agent Holder is awake and talking. His fellow agents are in there with him now, they said they would come out and let you know when they are finished. Hannah, he is going to be fine. Is there anything I can get for you?" He asks, knowing I had been through a lot and refused medical treatment when I was brought in earlier.

"No thank you, and thank you so much for everything that you have done for Declan." I lean in and give the doctor a quick hug.

The chief shakes the doctor's hand and thank him again. When he leaves the room I feel the weight of last night drain me of all of my strength. I sit down and weep into my hands, I am not able to contain all of my feelings anymore. For the first time since I pull the trigger, it really occurs to me that Mark's gone, no matter what happens he can never physically hurt me again. Now that I know that Quinn's safe and Declan's alive I can really take it all in.

"Hannah, I didn't tell them." Chief Duquette rubs my back as I cry.

I know that if the secret comes out it wouldn't be just me and Quinn affected, people lied to protect us, if that came out their reputations would be at risk too. The chief, the chief before him, the judge and the state's attorney were all a part of the cover-up, it would all come out. There isn't much I can do at this point, but I lift my head up and wipe my tears. There will be time to cry later; right now I need to be strong. I need to talk to Declan to tell him the truth, to show him the truth.

We only have to wait a little while longer, Agent Ridley comes into the room and sits down next to me. He takes my hand and tells me that I can go see Declan. He tells us that Declan was in and out of consciousness when they brought him in. He had lost a lot of blood but the bullet didn't hit any organs. They took him into surgery to clean up the internal bleeding and he should be fine.

I suppress a sigh of relief but wonder if he had told them the truth. I know he had been awake because I had seen him, he talked to me, but maybe he was in shock and just didn't remember. I thank Agent Ridley as he leads us to the room Declan's in. He lets us in and walks back down the hall leaving us standing in the open room with the injured Declan.

I look over at Declan who's laying in his hospital bed, he looks weak for the first time since I met him. There are machines all around him, lights blinking and something is beeping, I assume that's what they are supposed to do because no one seems concerned by the sounds. Declan smiles at me for a few moments and then pats the bed beside him. The sight of his smile still gives me butterflies. I walk over and stand beside the bed, not wanting to get too close and mess up any of the wires.

"I think yall owe me an explanation."

He doesn't seem upset but I can tell that he's hurt that I hadn't told him the truth about Quinn before, I know that I need to do it now, I owe him that much. I sit down on the bed next to him and look over at the chief, he nods as he takes the chair on the other side of the bed, allowing me to start the explanation but staying close for support.

"What I told Mark was true, I was pregnant with his child when my mother was murdered. We all devised a plan to keep it a secret, but you can

only hide a pregnancy for so long." I explain.

In fact, I couldn't hide my pregnancy at all, I realized right away that I had to protect the baby inside me, no one could know who its father was. I begged and pleaded for them to figure out a way to make that happen. Duquette was my advocate and got everyone else on board. They clearly made a mistake on who they chose to claim to be Quinn's father but it has worked out so far.

"We found a guy who was being charged with several drug offenses, with the help of the state's attorney's office we made him a deal. If he signed the paternal affidavit stating he was the baby's father, then agreed to sign his rights away they would look the other way on the more serious charges. He agreed and was sentenced to 30 days in the county jail. He was on day ten when he pissed off the wrong person, they took him out of his cell in a body bag." The chief continues.

I feel Declan's hand on mine again as he squeezes it reassuring me. I know the story, but I haven't heard it being told like this before. I was so young when it happened and no one likes to talk about it, in fact, we all swore that we would never talk about it to anyone. I feel the warm tears stream down my cheek, Declan reaches up and wipes them away. I don't deserve the understanding that this sweet man beside me is giving. I lied, we all lied. I have to remember that the lies weren't for me, they were for Quinn. Everything I do is for Quinn.

"Hannah, it's time we tell the truth about that night." The Chief looks at me thoughtfully.

I gasp, I mean I should have known this was coming, but I'm not ready. Am I? I mean it's Declan, we can trust him, right? I look at the chief again, and he just nods. I know he's right, so I take a deep breath, wipe the tears away from my eyes and tell the truth. The secret that has been left unspoken for eleven years.

Eleven Years Earlier

They were fighting again.

Inside the closet, I sat with my back pinned against the wall, my arms wrapped around my head, trying desperately to block out the noise. I didn't cry anymore as I used to years ago; I learned a long time ago it didn't help anyway. I sat hiding behind the hanging coats, seeking comfort in the light of the closet as I waited for them to stop, praying that it would be the last night he ever hit my mother.

The yelling stopped. My breath caught in my throat as I tried not to make a sound. Usually, the fights ended with a slamming door, had I missed it? I listened for a moment before slowly opening the closet door. I hoped the fight was finally over, but I wanted to be cautious in case it wasn't.

I had no sooner taken a suffocating breath of the heavy hallway air when I heard my mother yell again, this time she told him to just go ahead and pull the trigger. The memories of my dad came flooding back, my mother yelling at him to pull the trigger until he finally did.

I turned the corner expecting to see Mark with a gun to his head, threatening to end his own life. The excitement that I felt at the time scared me a little, but knowing that it could be the end of all the pain I was suffering was too good to be true. And it was. When I turned the corner I saw that the gun wasn't up against his head, it was instead pointed at my mother.

I didn't understand why my mother told him to pull the trigger, I knew that my mother was in love with this awful man and would never leave him no matter what he did to either of us. Is that why she wanted him to kill her, so she could finally break free?

When Mark noticed me standing over his wife's shoulder he lowered the gun. No matter how much he hated the woman in front of him he loved the girl behind her. He couldn't risk the bullet striking me too. He threw the gun onto the nearby table and began pacing the room. Thinking about what he should do.

I grabbed the gun, that was my chance to finally make the pain go away. I turned the gun on Mark, shaking as I raised it to shoot him right between the eyes. The eyes I had to look into every night as he raped me. The eyes that I hoped our unborn child growing inside me didn't inherit.

Just as I pulled the trigger my mother jumped in front of the gun. Protecting her abusive husband from her battered and broken daughter. The bullet went right through her skull, blood splattered everywhere. I didn't know what happened at first. I expected to see Mark on the floor, but he was standing there staring at me from where he stood a moment ago, I could feel his fear.

I looked at the gun in my blood-covered hands, then raised it again pulling the trigger over and over again pointing it directly at Mark's head. This time there were no gunshots and no blood. Just click after click. Mark was suddenly on top of me ripping the gun from my hands, he finally got it away from me he wiped my hands off on his shirt getting more blood all over me.

He told me to hide the gun. To go get back in the closet until the cops arrived. I did as he said. Taking the gun into the closet with me, I found an old coat on the way back and slid the gun into one of its inside pockets not bothering to wipe the blood off first. The closet felt suffocating all of a sudden, I couldn't stand being in there any longer. I pushed my way out and back into the room where my mother's lifeless body still lay in a puddle of her own blood.

I could hear the sirens coming from outside and could see the lights of the police cars as they tore into the driveway. I was still in a daze as the police broke down the door and stormed into the house. I expected to be tackled and handcuffed but instead found myself surrounded by paramedics.

When I turned to see where the cops were I found them tackling Mark to the ground and handcuffing him. They were arresting Mark for murdering my mother. I couldn't help but laugh. After everything he had done to us, he was being arrested for something he hadn't actually done. The laughter soon was mixed with sobs as I realized that he was going to tell them what really happened.

Officer Duquette came to my side and told me that I needed to go outside that I shouldn't see my mother that way. I was still laughing when he led me out to his patrol car. Once we were both in the car and he began to pull away from the house. About a mile down the road it hit me. I stopped laughing. I needed to know if they would let me raise my baby in prison.

The chief pulled the car over and told me to tell him everything that had happened that night. I told him everything from the fight to the time I pulled the trigger. He stared at me for a moment before asking me if Mark was the father. I didn't have to tell him, yes, he just knew. He told me that I was never allowed to tell anyone what I had just told him. He worked out the story and made me repeat it back to him. When anyone asked I was to tell them that Mark pulled the trigger. That I walked in right before it happened.

When I woke up in the hospital several hours later Mark had already been arrested, I told the story just like I had been told.

Declan

It's been six months since I was shot by Mark Patterson. I spent a week in the hospital and months after that doing physical therapy and mandatory counseling before being cleared to go back to work. During that time I had done a lot of thinking about Hannah's confession.

I was at a loss of how our justice system could be so flawed. The entire case went so wrong from the start. I have dedicated my entire life to catching bad guys and getting justice for the victims. But Hannah was the bad guy and the victim. How do I justify letting her get away with her crimes? How do I justify not?

After confessing what really happened to her mother, Hannah simply asked me to please consider keeping her secret and left the room. I haven't spoken to her since. I will never forget what the chief said before he left though. "Justice isn't always black and white. Sometimes in order to get real justice, you need to blur the lines. You have to look the other way. Sometimes the best thing you can do isn't always the right thing."

I have to admit the man did go above and beyond in this situation to protect a young girl and her baby, but he broke laws doing it. A man was sent to prison for a murder he didn't commit. The same man escaped and killed people who got in his way. Could those lives have been spared had they not lied over a decade ago? If they wouldn't have covered up Hannah's crime.

After six months I have decided it's time to talk to Hannah again. I look around the empty parking lot of the Oak Bend police department. It's mid-afternoon on a

Sunday and there doesn't appear to be many people out in town. I watch as a few cars drive by, none of them the one that I am waiting for.

I look at my phone again, I'm still a little early. I'll give her a few more minutes before I call I look up and see an officer has pulled into the lot. He looks familiar, I probably worked with him on the case, I just can't think of his name.

I really did enjoy working with the Oak Bend PD, they were a lot of help and very dedicated. I trust that a majority of them were left in the dark about most things and I respect that.

I catch movement out of the corner of my eye and see that two new vehicles have joined me. I assume one is Hannah's and the other one belongs to the former chief. I didn't ask him to come but I am not surprised he came anyway.

I heard that he retired shortly after the case closed, It was time but I have to wonder if the decision was made because Hannah had told me the truth. I wouldn't blame him either way.

I open my car door and step out into the cool Midwest air. Fall is coming hard this year and it looks like we are going to get some early snow.

"Agent Holder, thank you for coming. We can go inside and use a conference room to talk." He says shaking my hand.

I barely hear him because I am too busy staring at the woman coming up behind him. Her black hair blowing in the cool breeze, and those eyes making everything around them seem less significant. It's Hannah. My Hannah.

"That won't be necessary. I'm going to make this quick and clear."

I can see Hannah tense. I don't blame her, she's probably assuming the worst. I would be if I were her. She should be expecting it.

"Whatever you have decided to do I am prepared

to..." she starts, but I cut her off.

"Hannah don't, I came here today to tell you one thing. One thing that will change both of our lives." I pause and swallow hard. "Hannah, I have struggled with this for the last six months, I have spent countless sleepless nights wondering how I am going to do this, but I am just going to come out and say it, I am in love with you Hannah."

Hannah looks confused, but Chester lets out a loud laugh and leans up against his truck.

"Wow young man I mean I knew six months ago y'all loved each other but I had my doubts if you knew it. Hannah honey, breathe." He chuckles.

"I don't necessarily agree with how this whole thing was handled but I am sure that I love you and nothing we do now will change the past. So I am going to focus on the future which I hope will involve both of us together." I continue, still waiting for Hannah to react.

The reaction I got was a single tear falling down her cheek. I blew it. She doesn't love me, I was wrong. I make a move to leave when she takes a step towards me, slow at first then a little quicker. Suddenly she's in my arms, her lips against mine.

After a few moments, she pulls away and whispers "I love you too Agent Holder."

Dear readers,

Although Hannah's story is fictional, suicide, sexual assault, and domestic violence are very real. They are nightmares that real-life people experience every day. Nightmares that I have personally experienced.

When I was a little girl my father struggled with depression, he fought the battle alone and ended up taking his own life. My mother remarried rather quickly, and we went on with our lives. Throughout the years we had some hard times, as most people do, but overall, I remember being loved.

When I was fourteen things changed. My mother's husband started taking a new interest in me. It wasn't long after that when the true nightmare began. One morning something inside of him snapped. He murdered my mother in her sleep then came into my bedroom and sexually assaulted me before calling the police on himself.

For years following these events, I had reoccurring nightmares about him escaping from prison and trying to find me. Those nightmares gave me the idea for this book.

My hope is to spread awareness about these very real issues using my tales of fiction.

Remember, you are loved, you are not alone, and I believe you.

Amanda Sowers

Domestic Violence Hotline
800-799-SAFE

Sexual Assault Hotline
800-656-HOPE

Suicide Prevention Hotline
800-273-TALK

Acknowledgments

I would like to thank everyone who has taken the time to follow me on this journey.

Special thank you to Darci, Ben, Debbie, and Cathi for reading through my mess of a manuscript on multiple occasions. Thank you for pointing out all of my mistakes.

I should also thank my daughter Serenity, who probably didn't even realize I was writing a book most of the time because the YouTube is way more exciting than me. Except of course when I was reading it aloud and she told me that it was annoying. Thanks again for the support.

Thank you to Q Design for the amazing cover, I appreciate the time and talent you put into making it perfect.

Last but not least I need to thank my best friend Katy who supports me every day by insulting me and keeping my ego in check. Those daily jokes about my dead mom really made this story what it is. Thank you for being you, don't ever change.

About The Author

Amanda Sowers was born and raised in the Midwest. She currently resides in South Dakota with her daughter, her dog and three cats. She spends her days working as a customer service representative and her evenings plotting people's murders, for book purposes of course.

Having experienced childhood trauma, she has a passion for spreading awareness for domestic violence, suicide, and sexual assault prevention. Through her tales of mystery and suspense she hopes to shine light on these very real issues and maybe even change someone's life.

Made in the USA
Coppell, TX
09 March 2020